THIRTY INDIAN LEGENDS OF CANADA

THIRTY INDIAN LEGENDS OF CANADA

By Margaret Bemister

Illustrations by Douglas Tait

J.J. Douglas Ltd.
Vancouver

First published by Macmillan Company of Canada, Ltd., 1917
First J. J. Douglas Ltd. edition, 1973
New impression 1979

Canadian Shared Cataloguing in Publication Data

Bemister, Margaret, 1877—
Thirty Indian Legends of Canada

1. Indians of North America — Canada — Legends. I. Title

E78.C2B45 398.2'09701
ISBN 0-88894-025-4
Library of Congress catalog card number 74-160452

J. J. Douglas Ltd.
1875 Welch Street
North Vancouver, British Columbia

Designed by Jim Rimmer
Typography by Vancouver Typesetting Co. Ltd.
Printed and bound in Canada

Preface

For the most part the legends here told are drawn from original sources. Many of the stories are printed for the first time; others have been adapted from well-known authorities. The author wishes to acknowledge in this latter connection help received from the collection, "The Indian in his Wigwam." Thanks are also due to Mr. G. H. Gunn, St. Andrew's Locks, Manitoba, for the "Sleep Fairies"; to Mr. C. Linklater, Portage la Prairie, Manitoba, for the "Adventures of Wesakchak"; to Mr. J. S. Logie, Summerland, British Columbia, for "The Chief's Bride"; to the Okanagan chief, Antowyne, for the other Okanagan legends; and to a paper read before the Royal Society of Canada by Mr. G. M. Dawson, for "The Old Stump".

Winnipeg, Canada
September 15, 1912

Contents

PAGE

Preface . . . 3
Contents . . . 5
The Giant Bear . . . 7
The Summer-Maker . . . 15
The Sleep Fairies . . . 20
Shingebiss . . . 26
The Queer Little Animal . . . 29
The Dormouse . . . 33
The Windmaker . . . 38
Moowis . . . 44
The Daughters of the Star . . . 47
Koto and the Bird . . . 51
The Humpbacked Manitou . . . 56
The Tribe that Grew Out of a Shell . . . 60
The Story of the Indian Corn . . . 64
The Magician of Lake Huron . . . 67
The Fairies' Cliff . . . 71
The Stone Canoe . . . 75
The White Feather . . . 79
The Lone Lightning . . . 85
The Enchanted Moccasins . . . 87
The Five Water-Spirits . . . 92

PAGE

The Canoe Breaker 94

The Old Stump 98

The Cliff of Sinikielt 103

The Strange Dream 108

Big Chief's Conquest 112

The Red Swan 117

The Whispering Grass 123

The Legend of Mackinac Island 130

The Adventures of Wesakchak 132

The Wonderful Ball

A Wonderful Journey

The Further Adventures of Wesakchak 141

The Grey Goose

Little Brother Rabbit

The Bald-headed Eagles

Pronouncing Vocabulary 152

The Giant Bear

In the far north there was a village where many warlike Indians lived. In one family there were ten brothers, all brave and fearless. In the spring of the year the youngest brother blackened his face and fasted for several days. Then he sent for his nine brothers and said to them:

"I have fasted and dreamed, and my dreams are good. Will you come on a war journey with me?"

"Yes," they all said readily.

"Then tell no one, not even your wives, of our plan." They agreed to meet on a certain night so that no one should see them go. One brother was named Mudjekeewis, and he was very odd. He was the first to promise that he would not tell. The next two days were spent in preparations for the journey. Mudjekeewis told his wife many times to get his moccasins for him.

"And hurry," he said; "do hurry."

"Why do you want them?" she asked. "You have a good pair on."

"Well, if you must know, we are going on a war journey," he answered.

When the night had come which the leader had named, they met at his wigwam and set out on their long journey. The snow lay on the ground, and the night was very dark.

After they had travelled some miles, the leader gathered some snow and made it into a ball. He threw it in the air and said, as it fell, "It was thus I saw the snow fall in my dreams to cover our footmarks, so that no one may follow us."

The snow began to fall heavily and continued for two days. It was so thick that they could scarcely see each other, though they walked very closely together.

The leader cheered his brothers by telling them they would win in their battle. At this Mudjekeewis, who was walking behind, ran forward. He swung his war-club in the air and uttered the war-cry. Then bringing his war-club down, he struck a tree, and it fell as if hit by lightning.

"See brothers," he said, "this is the way I shall serve our enemy."

"Hush, Mudjekeewis," said the leader. "He whom we are going to fight cannot be treated so lightly."

Then they travelled on for several days, until at last they reached the borders of the White Plain, where the bones of men lay bleaching.

"These are the bones of men who have gone before us. No one has ever returned to tell of their sad fate." Mudjekeewis looked frightened at this and thought, "I wonder who this terrible enemy is."

"Be not afraid, my brothers," said the leader. Mudjekeewis then took courage, again jumped forward, and uttering the war-cry, brought his war-club down on a small rock, and split it into pieces. "See, I am not afraid," he cried. "Thus shall I serve my enemy." But the leader still pressed onward over the plain, until at last a small rise in the ground brought them in sight of the enemy. Some distance away, on the top of the mountain, a giant bear lay sleeping.

"Look, brothers," said the leader. "There is the mighty enemy, for he is a Manitou.[1] But come now, we need not fear, as he is asleep. Around his neck he has the precious wampum,[2] which we must take from him."

They advanced slowly and quietly. The huge animal did not hear them. Around his neck was a belt which contained the wampum.

"Now we must take this off," said the youngest brother. One after the other tried, but could not do it, until the next to the youngest tried. He pulled it nearly over the bear's head. Then came the turn of the youngest, and he pulled it the rest of the way. He put the belt quickly on the back of the oldest brother.

"Now we must run," said the leader, "for when he awakens,

---

[1] A manitou is the spirit of an Indian who has been killed. Manitous often take the forms of animals when they come back to life.

[2] Wampum; long, narrow beads, sometimes made of shells. They were usually blue and white and were often woven into a belt. They were greatly treasured by the Indians.

he will miss his belt."

They all hastened away. The wampum was very heavy, so they had to take turns carrying it. They kept looking back as they ran, and had almost reached the edge of the plain before the bear awoke. He slowly rose to his feet and stood for a moment before he noticed that the belt was gone. Then he uttered a roar that reached to the skies.

"Who has dared to steal my belt?" he roared. "Earth is not so large but that I shall find him."

Saying this, he jumped from the mountain, and the earth shook with his weight. Then with powerful strides he rushed in pursuit of the brothers.

They had passed all the bones now and were becoming very tired.

"Brothers," said the leader, "I dreamed that when we were hard pressed and running for our lives we saw a lodge where an old man lived, and he helped us. I hope my dream will come true."

Just then they saw, a short distance away, a lodge with smoke curling from the top. They ran to it, and an old man opened the door.

"Grandfather," they gasped, "will you save us? A Manitou is after us."

"Who is a Manitou but I?" said he. "Come in and eat." They entered the lodge and he gave them food. Then, opening the door, he looked out and saw the bear coming with great strides. Shutting the door, he said, "He is indeed a mighty Manitou and will take my life; but you asked for my help and I shall give it. When he comes, you run out of the back door."

Going to a bag which hung from a tree, he took out two small black dogs. He patted the sides of the dogs, and they began to swell until they filled the doorway. The dogs had strong, white teeth and growled fiercely. The bear had now reached the door, and with one bound the first dog leaped out, followed by the second. The brothers ran out of the back of the lodge. They could hear the howls of the animals as they fought, and looking back, they saw first one dog killed, then the other, and at last the shrieks of the old man came to them as the bear tore him in pieces. They doubled their speed now, as they saw the bear beginning to follow them again. The food they had eaten gave them new strength, so they were able to run very swiftly for a time. But at last they all felt their strength fail again, for the bear was close behind them now.

"Brothers, I had another dream," said the leader. "It was that an old Manitou saved us. Perhaps his lodge is near us now."

Even as he spoke, they came in sight of another lodge, and as they ran up to the door an old man opened it.

"Save us from the Manitou," they cried as they rushed in.

"Manitou?" he said. "Who is a Manitou but I? Come in and eat," and he closed the door. He brought food for them; then he looked out of the door. The bear was only a few yards away now. Hastily closing the door, he said, "This is indeed a mighty Manitou. You have brought trouble to me, my children; but you run out the back way and I shall fight him."

He then went to his medicine sack and drew out two war-clubs of black stone. As he handled them they grew to an immense size. He opened the door, and as he did so, the brothers ran out the back way. They could hear the blows like claps of thunder as he hit the bear on the head. After that came two sharp cracks, and they knew the clubs were broken with the force of the blows. Then came his shrieks, as he met the fate of the first old man. They tried to run faster than ever now, for they knew the bear must be after them again, but their strength was nearly gone.

"Oh, brother," they asked, "have you no other dream to help us?"

"Yes, I dreamed, when we were running like this, that we came to a lake and on the shore of it was a canoe with ten paddles in it waiting for us. We jumped in and were saved."

As he spoke, there appeared in front of them a lake just as he had dreamed, and a canoe waiting. Getting in, they quickly paddled to the middle of the lake, and waited to see what the bear would do.

He came on with his slow, powerful strides until he reached the water's edge. Then, rising on his hind legs, he took a look around. Dropping down, he waded into the water, but slipped and nearly fell. He waded out and began to walk around the lake. When he reached the spot he had started from, he bent down his head and began to drink the waters of the lake. He drank in such large mouthfuls that the brothers could see the water sinking, and the current began to flow so swiftly towards his mouth that they could not keep their canoe steady. It floated in the current straight to him.

"Now, Mudjekeewis," said the leader, "this is your chance to show us how you would treat your enemy."

"I shall show you and him," said Mudjekeewis.

Then, as the canoe came near the big mouth, he stood up and levelled his war-club. Just as the boat touched the bear's teeth, Mudjekeewis uttered the war-cry and dealt the animal a mighty blow on the head. This he repeated, and the bear fell stunned. As the animal fell, he disgorged the water with such force that it sent the canoe spinning to the other side of the lake, where the brothers landed and ran ahead as fast as they could. They had not gone far when they could hear the bear coming behind them.

"Do not be afraid, brothers," said the leader, as he noticed how frightened they all looked. "I have one more dream. If it fails us, we are lost, but let us hope that it will come true. I dreamed we were running, and we came to a lodge out of which came a young maiden. Her brother was a Manitou and by his magic she saved us. Run on and fear not, else your limbs will be fear-bound. Look for his lodge."

And sure enough, behind a little clump of trees, stood a lodge. As they ran to it a maiden came forth and invited them in.

"Enter," she said, "and rest. I shall meet the bear, and when I need you, I shall call you."

Saying this, she took down a medicine-sack, which was hanging on the wall near the door. They entered, and she walked out to meet the bear. The animal came up with angry growls and swinging strides. The maiden quickly opened the medicine-sack and took out some war feathers, paint, and tufts of hair.

As the bear came up, the girl tossed them up in the air, saying, "Behold, these are the magic arrows of my dead brother. These are the magic war paints of my dead brother. This is the eagle's feather of my dead brother, and these are the tufts of hair of wild animals he has killed."

As she said these words and the things fell on the ground near the animal, he tottered and fell. She called the brothers, and they rushed out.

"Cut him into pieces quickly," she said, "or he will come to life again."

They all set to work and cut the huge animal into small pieces, which they tossed away. When they had finished, they saw, to their surprise, that these pieces had turned into small, black bears, which had jumped up and were running away in every direction. And it is from these bears that the bears called the Makwas had their beginning.

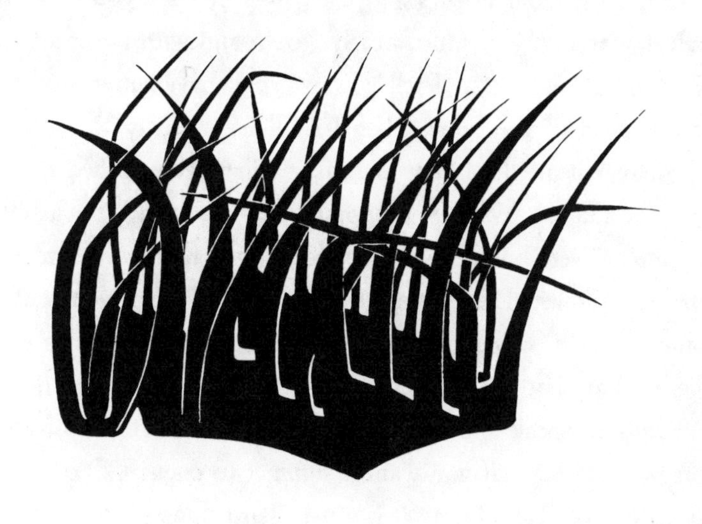

The Summer Maker

ONCE in the far north there lived a Manitou whose name was Ojeeg, or the fisher. He and his wife and one son lived on the shore of a lake and were very happy together.

In that country there was never any spring or summer, and the snow lay deep on the ground all the year round. But this did not daunt the fisher. He went forth every day and always brought back plenty of game.

The son wished to be a great hunter like his father, so he often took his bow and arrows and went out to kill birds. But he nearly always returned with benumbed hands and crying with cold.

One day, as he was returning, feeling very discouraged and ready to cry, he noticed a red squirrel on the top of a tree. As he reached for his arrows to shoot him, the squirrel spoke:

"Put away your arrows and listen to me. I see you go forth each day and always return nearly frozen and with never a bird. Now, if you will do as I tell you, we shall have summer all the time instead of the snow. Then I shall have plenty to eat, and you may kill all the birds you wish. When you go home, you must cry and sob. When your mother asks you what is the matter, do not answer, but throw away your bow and arrow and cry harder than ever. Do not eat any supper, and when your father comes home, he will ask your mother what is the matter with you. She will say that she does not know, that you only sob and cry, and will not speak. When he asks you to give the reason of your sorrow, tell him that you want a summer to come. Coax him to get it for you. He will say it is a very hard thing to do, but will promise to try. Now remember all this and do as I tell you."

As the squirrel finished speaking, he disappeared, and the son returned home. Everything happened as the little squirrel had said, and when the son asked his father to get summer for him, Ojeeg replied, "My son, this is a hard task you have given me. But I love you and so shall try for your sake. It may cost me my life, but I shall do my best."

Then he called together all his friends, and they had a feast. A bear was killed and roasted, and they arranged to meet on Thursday to begin their journey.

When the day came, they all gathered; there was the otter, the beaver, the lynx, and the wolverine. Ojeeg said good-bye to his wife and son, and the party set out. For twenty days they travelled through the snow, and at last came to the foot of a mountain. The animals were all very tired by this time, all but Ojeeg. He was a nimble little animal and used to long journeys.

As they began to go up the mountain, they noticed footprints and marks of blood, as if some hunter had gone before them with an animal he had killed.

"Let us follow these tracks," said the fisherman, "and see if we can get something to eat."

When they reached the top of the mountain, they noticed a small lodge.

"Now be very careful and do not laugh at anything we see," said Ojeeg.

They knocked at the door, and it was opened by a very strange man. He had a huge head, big strong teeth, and no arms. He invited them to come in and eat. There was meat cooking in a wooden pot on the fire. The man lifted it off when they were not looking, and gave them all something to eat. They wondered how he could do this, and how he had killed the animal, but they soon learned the secret. He was a Manitou!

As they were eating, the otter began to laugh at the strange movements of the Manitou, who, hearing a noise, turned quickly and threw himself on the otter. He was going to smother him, as this was his way of killing animals. But the otter managed to wriggle from under him, and escaped out of the door.

The rest remained there for the night. When they were going in the morning, the Manitou told them what path to take and what to do when they reached the right spot. They thanked him and started on again.

For twenty more days they travelled, and then they reached another mountain. They climbed to the top of this, and they knew by certain signs it was the spot the Manitou had described. So they seated themselves in a circle and filled their pipes. They pointed to the sky, the four winds, and the earth; then they began to smoke. As they looked up at the sky they were silent with awe, for they were on such a high mountain that the sky seemed only a few yards off. They then prepared themselves, and Ojeeg told the otter to have the first trial at making a hole in the sky. With a grin the otter consented. He made a spring, but fell down the side of the hill. The snow was moist, so he slid all the way to the bottom. When he had picked himself up, he cried, "This is the last time I shall make such a jump; I am going home," and away he went. The beaver had the next turn, but did no better. The lynx had no better luck. Then came the turn of the wolverine.

"Now," said Ojeeg to him, "I am going to depend on you; you are brave and will try again and again."

So the wolverine took a jump, and the first time nearly reached the sky; the second time he cracked it, and the third time he made a hole and crawled in. Ojeeg nimbly followed, and they found themselves on a beautiful, green plain. Lovely shade trees grew at some distance, and among the trees were rivers and lakes. On the water floated all kinds of water-fowl. Then they noticed long lodges. They were empty, except for a great many cages filled with beautiful birds. The spirits who lived in these lodges were wandering among the trees. As Ojeeg noticed the birds, he remembered his son. He quickly opened the doors of the cages, and the birds rushed out. They flew through the air and down through the opening in the sky.

The warm winds, that always blow in that heavenly place, followed the birds down through the opening and began to melt the snows of the north. Then the guardian spirits noticed what was happening and ran with great shouts to the spot where all were escaping. But Spring and Summer had nearly gone. They struck a great blow and cut Summer in two, so that only part of it reached the earth. The wolverine heard the noise and raced for the hole, getting through before they could close it. But the fisher was farther away and could not reach the hole in time. The spirits closed up the opening and turned to catch him. He ran over the plains to the north, going so fast that he gained the trees before they could catch him. He quickly climbed the largest one, and they began to shoot at him with their arrows.

There was only one place in the fisher's body where he could be hurt, — a spot near the tip of his tail; so the spirits kept shooting a long time before an arrow struck that spot. At last one did, and he fell to the ground. As it was now nearly night, the spirits went back to their lodges and left him there alone. He stretched out his limbs and said:

"I have kept my promise to my son, though it has cost me my life. But I shall always be remembered by the natives of the earth, and I am happy to think of the good I have sent them. From now on they will have different seasons, and eight to ten moons without snow."

In the morning they found him lying dead with the arrow through his tail, and to this day he may be seen in the northern sky.

The Sleep Fairies

A HUNTER was once going through a forest with his dogs. After he had gone some distance he missed them. He called and whistled, but they did not come, so he turned back to find them. Going some distance farther, he thought he saw one lying under some low bushes, and when he reached the spot, he saw his three dogs lying there fast asleep. He tried to waken them, but they would open their eyes only for a moment, then fall asleep again. Soon he began to feel a strange, sleepy feeling coming over him. He shook himself and tried to keep awake. Just then he noticed a very large insect on a branch of a tree. It had many wings on its back, which kept up a steady, droning noise. When it noticed the hunter looking at it, the insect said, "I am Weeng, the spirit of sleep. Your dogs came too near my home, and so they have fallen under my spell. In a few minutes you will be asleep yourself."

"Must I go to sleep?" said the hunter. "I would like to go back to my lodge."

"You are a brave chief and have always been kind to the forest insects, so this time I am going to let you go. Take a leaf from yonder little tree, chew it and swallow the juice."

The hunter did as he was told and at once the sleepy feeling was gone. Then the strangest thing happened. He saw all around him queer, little fairies, each one with a tiny war-club. They peeped from out the bark of the trees, from amidst the grass, and even from out his pouch.

"What are these?" he asked Weeng.

"They are my sleep fairies, and are called 'Weengs.' Now you may waken your dogs and go." And before the hunter had time to reply the insect had gone.

He turned and roused the dogs, who followed him, still looking very stupid. As he went he saw the Weengs all around the trees, and many seemed to be coming with him. When he reached his lodge, he saw the little creatures run to the men and climb up their foreheads; then with their war-clubs they began to knock them on the head. Soon the Indians began to yawn and rub their eyes, and in a little while they all lay asleep.

Then the hunter began to feel his own head grow heavy. He tried to keep awake, but could not, so he stretched himself beside the fire and went to sleep. When he awakened and looked around, there were no fairies to be seen.

The hunter determined to go into the forest and see if he could find the little tree from which he had plucked the leaf. But before he went, he carefully tied up his dogs, for he did not wish them to follow him and again fall under the spell of Weeng. They whined when he left them and pulled at their ropes, but he was soon lost to their sight among the trees. Making his way slowly through the forest, he kept a sharp lookout for the little tree with the magic leaves. But he could see nothing that looked like it. For many hours he tramped on, and at last he threw himself down on the ground to rest.

As he lay there, he heard a droning noise above his head. He looked up quickly, and there sat Weeng on the farthermost branch of the tree.

"Good-morning, great hunter," said the insect. "You have been searching for my little tree, have you not?"

"Yes," replied the hunter. "How did you know?"

"I know many things," said Weeng; "but listen, to me. Yonder is the tree." As he spoke, he pointed to a little tree not two yards away. "Pluck one of the leaves, but do not chew it until sunset. At that hour I utter my sleep call, which bids all the insects fly home to rest. When you hear the call, you may chew the leaf, for I want you to see what happens then."

"Is anything strange going to happen?" asked the hunter.

"Great hunter," said Weeng, "if you will remain in this forest behind that large oak tree, you may see it all. One hour before sunset, the Red Squirrel and all his army are coming to attack me."

"Why are they going to do that?" asked the hunter, in surprise.

"Because the Red Squirrel wishes to have my branch for his home. He ordered me to get down, and I refused. So, one hour before sunset, he and his army are coming to drive me from my home."

"What are you going to do?" asked the hunter. "Can I help you?"

"I and my winged friends," said Weeng, "are going to fight them when they come. Yes, great hunter, you can help us by remaining to see that the battle is fair. The Red Squirrel knows that if he can once touch me, I must fall. But my insects have sharp swords, and they can keep the army back till sunset."

"And what will happen them?" asked the hunter.

"Then the insects must go to their homes. But if you swallow the juice of the leaf, you will see the end of the battle. Now go and hide behind the oak tree. In a few minutes my army will be here."

The hunter did as he was bidden and took his place behind the tree. From here he could see Weeng quite plainly, but he was himself hidden. In a few minutes the insects began to assemble. First came the wasps, looking fierce and warlike. Then came the bees, buzzing along with indignation. Then dozens of flies, blue-bottles, sand-flies, and bull-flies, all ready for the fight. Then followed the moths, ladybugs, butterflies, and mosquitoes.

Lastly, with a great noise, came a regiment of hornets and took their places on the branch directly in front of Weeng. The others had gathered in a huge circle around him, and in the midst of the bodyguard he sat, like a general ready for the attack of the enemy. He had not long to wait, for somewhere in the forest the Red Squirrel had assembled his army, and now he brought them forward in one body to the foot of the tree. All the red squirrels were in front, next came the gray squirrels, then the chipmunks.

The Red Squirrel gave the command, and up the tree his army began to climb. Out on the branch they came, where Weeng sat at the farthest end. But the hornets were ready for them, and as they advanced the sharp swords of the defenders pricked their noses, eyes and bodies. Backward they tumbled, some falling from the limb, others clinging desperately to the under side. Then the gray squirrels pushed forward, and in spite of many wounds, broke through the ranks of the hornets. They had nearly reached Weeng when the bees, buzzing more indignantly than ever, made one fierce dash at them. They gray squirrels fought bravely, but at every turn they met terrible, stinging blows. At last they could not see what they were doing, and, like the red squirrels, many of them fell from the limb.

While this part of the battle was going on, the chipmunks had been waging a war of their own with the wasps, who had attacked them. The battle had been a sharp one, and many soldiers of both armies lay dead on the ground below the tree. But the chipmunks had won the victory, and now made their way along the branches towards Weeng. Their leader, a large, bold-looking chipmunk, made a fierce rush at Weeng, and almost touched him. But just as he did so, with a noiseless swoop, down came the mosquitoes upon him. They covered his head, until not a part of it was to be seen. He slapped wildly at them, lost his hold on the branch, and fell to the ground. With redoubled fury on rushed the other chipmunks and the red squirrels, who had by this time recovered. They were met by a solid wall of insects bristling with sharp swords, for the wasps, the hornets, and flies had placed themselves across their path. Then came the hottest part of the battle, and in one confused mass they struggled and fought on the slender branch. In the midst if this there sounded a soft, sweet call. It was the sleep call of the fairy Weeng. At once all the insects sheathed their swords, and turning, fluttered slowly home to bed. As each one departed, he uttered a soft good-night to Weeng.

The hunter, who was watching all this anxiously, wondered that although the Red Squirrel's army was still fighting it was making no headway. He wondered how this could be. Suddenly he remembered the leaf in his pocket. At once he chewed it, and he then saw the reason for the squirrels' defeat. At the call of Weeng his sleep fairies had come forth, and now with their clubs were knocking their enemies on the head. Blow after blow they struck. The squirrels resisted bravely, but it was useless. In a few minutes they were driven back and off the branch of the tree, and were glad to escape to their homes. As the darkness gathered and the magic of the leaf began to wear away, the hunter could just dimly see Weeng sitting in the midst of his sleep fairies, like a great general who has won his battle.

Shingebiss

ONCE there was a little duck, whose name was Shingebiss. He lived by himself in a small lodge, and was very contented and happy. This lodge was built on the shore of a lake. When the cold winter days came, and the lake was frozen over, all the other ducks flew away to a warmer land. But Shingebiss was not afraid of the cold. He gathered four large logs and took them into his lodge. Each log was big enough to burn for a month, and as there were only four cold months, there would be enough to last him through the winter.

Then each morning he would go to the lake, and hunt for places where the rushes came through the ice. He would pull these out with his strong beak, and catch fish through the openings.

Kabibonokka, the north wind, saw him, and said to himself, "What a strange person this is. He sings and is out on the coldest days. But I shall stop his singing."

So he blew a cold blast from the north-west, which froze the ice on the lake much deeper. Still Shingebiss came out in the morning, caught his fish, and went home singing.

"How strange," said the north wind, "I cannot freeze him; I shall go and visit his lodge. Perhaps I can put out his fire."

So he went and knocked at the door of the lodge. Shingebiss was within. He had cooked and eaten his fish, and now was lying on one side in front of the fire, singing a song. He heard the north wind at the door, but he pretended that he did not. He went on singing in quite a loud voice:

"Windy god, I know your plan,
You are but my fellow-man.
Blow you may your coldest breeze,
Shingebiss you cannot freeze;
Sweep the strongest wind you can,
Shingebiss is still your man.
Heigh, for life — ho, for bliss,
Who so free as Shingebiss?"

The north wind heard him and was very angry. He blew his coldest blast under the doorway. Shingebiss felt it, but still went on singing. Then the north wind opened the door, and walked in. He took a seat beside the fire, and Shingebiss pretended not to see him. He just went on singing, and after a while took his poker and stirred the logs. This made them blaze brightly, and in a few minutes tears began to run down Kabibonokka's cheeks. He pushed his chair away from the fire and tried to blow his icy breath on the blazing log. But the warm air pushed the cold breeze back and wrapped Kabibonokka around like a cloak. The tears were running in streams down his cheeks now, and the heavy frost on his long beard and hair melted and made pools of water on the floor. He could stand it no longer. Rising, he hastily passed out the door, saying to himself, "I cannot put out his fire, but I shall freeze the lake so deep that he will not be able to catch any more fish."

So that night he blew his coldest breath. Next morning the ice on the lake was very thick. Brave little Shingebiss went from one place to another, trying to find a thin spot. At last a bunch of rushes came out as he pulled, and, looking in the hole, he saw several fine fish. He sang merrily as he caught them, and the north wind heard the song. Looking out of his lodge, he saw what Shingebiss was doing. At first he was very angry, then he began to feel afraid.

"This duck must be helped by some Manitou," he said. "I shall leave him in peace after this."

Then Kabibonokka went in and closed his lodge door and Shingebiss never saw him again.

The Queer Little Animal

An Indian was once wandering across the prairie. He was tired and hungry and very lonely, too, for he had not seen a human being for many weeks. He lay down on the ground and fell asleep. While he was lying there, he dreamed that a small voice said, "My grandson," to him. He wakened with a start and again heard the voice. It came from the grass near him, but he could see nothing.

"Pick me up," said the voice, "and I shall be your friend forever. Put me in your belt and never lay me aside, and you will always have success."

The Indian looked closely in the grass and saw a tiny creature. It was about the size of a baby mouse, and had no hair on its skin excepting a little bunch on the tip of its tail. He picked it up and sewed it in his belt. Then he travelled on until he came to a village where a tribe of Indians lived. A broad road ran through the centre of the village, but the strange thing was, that the lodges on one side of the road were empty, while those on the other side were filled with Indians. He walked boldly into the village. The people ran out to meet him, crying, "Here is the being of whom we have heard so much. Welcome, Anishinaba."

The chief's son was very kind to him and took him to his father's lodge. The people of this tribe spent most of their time in games and trials of strength. The trial they liked best was called The Freezing Water Trial; that was, they had to lie down in icy, cold water and let it freeze around them. The man who could stay the longest was considered the bravest. The next night they asked Anishinaba to try the test with them. He was quite willing and went with them to the place where the test was to be made. He kept on his belt, and so felt very comfortable, for the little animal made everything easy for him. The water began to freeze and the Indians called out, "How are you feeling?" He did not answer them.

About midnight, he noticed they had stopped talking. He called out, "How are you feeling now? I am very warm." They did not answer him, so he arose and walked to where they were lying. They were frozen stiff. He went back to the camp and told the other Indians. Everybody declared that he was the bravest warrior, since he had not been frozen. The chief was so pleased with him that he gave him his daughter. The Indians went to fetch the bodies of the frozen men, but were surprised to find them changed into buffaloes. These animals went to live in the other side of the village; and after that, every one Anishinaba killed was changed into some kind of an animal and went into that part of the village to live. Very shortly the empty lodges were filled.

One day Anishinaba lay down on the grass to have a sleep. He had taken off his belt, and it lay in the long grass beside him. When he wakened, he forgot about it. This was the first time he had ever gone without the little animal since he came to the village. That night some Indians who were unfriendly to him asked him to try the freezing trial again. He consented, for he was not at all afraid. But still he did not think of his belt, and so the freezing water benumbed his body and in a short time he was frozen stiff. His enemies then cut his body into many pieces and scattered them over the village. His wife wept bitterly for many days. Then suddenly she remembered his belt, and went in search of it. She found it in the grass where he had slept. As she picked it up, the tiny voice said, "Unpin me." She opened the little seam where the animal lay and out he came. He began to shake himself, and at each shake grew larger, until at last he was the size of a small dog.

The queer-looking animal ran away then as fast as he could go. All around the village he went, gathering up the pieces of his master's body. When he had them gathered, he laid them together in their right places. Then he uttered a loud howl, and the pieces joined together. He uttered another, and the body began to breathe. Then he uttered one that reached to the skies, and his master arose and stood before him. The animal then spoke. "You should not have parted with me," he said. "That was why you lost your life. Now, I shall reveal myself to you." He began shaking himself like a dog, and at each shake he grew larger, until at last he was immense. Then a long snout grew from his head, and two big, shining teeth from his mouth. His skin was still smooth, without one hair excepting the bunch on the end of his tail.

"I am going to give my gift to you," said the wild boar. "After this you shall live on the meat of animals, instead of the animals eating you. But you and all mankind must respect me and must not eat my flesh nor that of any of my kind."

The Dormouse

MANY years ago the animals ruled the earth. They had killed every one but a brother and a sister. These two lived in a lodge far away in the forest, where the animals could not find them. The boy was a tiny, little fellow, — he had never grown any larger than a baby, — so the girl had to do all the work. Each day she would go out into the bush and gather wood for the lodge fire. She always took her brother with her, for he was too small to leave alone. A big bird might fly away with him.

One day she gave him a little bow and arrows, and said, "You stay here while I take the wood home. When the snow-birds come to get the worms out of the wood, see if you can shoot one." So she went home and left him. He did not come until nearly evening. He looked very sad and tired, for he had been unable to shoot even one bird.

"Never mind," said the sister, kindly. "Try again to-morrow."

The next day he went again with her, and when he came back in the evening, he said, "I shot this bird, and now, sister, strip the skin off it, stretch, and cure it. Then when I have killed enough birds, I shall have a coat made of the skins." At last when he had ten skins, his sister made him a coat of them. He was to tiny that it fitted him nicely. Of course he was very proud of it.

One day he said, "Sister, is there no one living in this world except ourselves?"

"Yes," she answered. "Many miles from here live the animals we are afraid of. But never go near their village, for they will kill you."

"Oh, I am not afraid," he said; and in spite of all her coaxing he made ready to go on his journey.

One morning he set out, and by noon had walked quite a distance. He felt very tired and threw himself down on a plot of grass where the sun had melted the snow. He fell asleep, and while he was lying there the hot sun dried the skins of his bird coat. When he awoke, he felt as though he were buttoned up in a coat much too small for him.

He was very angry at the sun, for he knew it had done this. "I shall punish you," he cried up to it. "You think you are so high up there, and I am so small, that you do not care, but I shall show you."

Then he went home to his sister and showed her the coat, and told her all about it. She begged him not to feel so angry. He would not listen to her, but went and lay down on the bed. For ten days he stayed there without eating a bite. Then he turned over on his other side and lay for ten days more.

At last he arose and said, "Sister, please make me a snare. I want to catch the sun." She told him she had nothing with which to make the snare. He nearly cried when she said this. Then she remembered some bits of deer sinew that were in the lodge. She made a snare of this, but he said, "That will not do," and began to cry again. Then she asked him if her hair would do.

"No, it will not," he said.

"Well, I have nothing else," she told him, and went out of the lodge. She thought and thought, and at last she said to herself, "I shall use my hair, and perhaps he will never know." So she made a snare like the one used to catch moose. When she took it in to him, and asked, "Will this do?" he looked very pleased, and said, "Oh, yes, that is the very thing." He took it, and drew the threads through his lips. They changed at once into red, metal cords, which he wound around his waist.

Then he made ready for his journey, and about midnight he set out. He walked on for a long time, until he came to the spot where the sun came up. He fixed the snare, and then hid behind some bushes. In a little while the sun began to rise, and was at once caught in the snare.

The animals, who ruled the earth, were greatly excited because the morning did not come. They knew it was time for the sun to be up, so they called a council.

"What is to be done?" asked the bear.

"Some one must go and see what has happened," replied the wolf.

"Let the dormouse go," said the beaver, "as he is the largest of us all."

In those days the dormouse was very large. He looked like a

mountain when he stood up.

"Yes," said the wolf, "let the dormouse go. He is proud of his size and his strength. Let him show us what he can do when there is danger before him."

They all looked around for the dormouse, but there was no sign of him.

"He thinks that we shall send him to find the sun," said the fox. "He is afraid and has hidden himself."

"Not so," returned the beaver. "The dormouse is not a coward. Let us call him. He cannot be far away."

With that, they all began to call the dormouse. In a moment there was a crackling of branches and the sound of heavy footsteps, and a huge figure loomed up in the darkness.

"Brother dormouse," said the fox, "you are so brave that we have chosen you to go in search of the sun. What is your answer?"

"I am quite ready to go," replied the dormouse, "and if I cannot find the sun and send it to you, I shall not return myself."

At once the dormouse started towards the sun. As he came close to it, the hot rays began to burn his back, but he kept on, and began to chew the cords, which bound it. In a few minutes the top of his back was a heap of ashes, and he felt himself shrivelling with the heat. He kept on bravely, and at last the cords were sundered and the sun free. But by this time the dormouse was a very small animal, and has remained so ever since.

All this time the brother, who was lying hidden, had been watching what was happening. As the dormouse began to smoke, he grew a little frightened, and when it began to shrivel he was terrified. All he wished for was to escape from this glaring sun, which surely would quickly consume him too.

Lying flat on the ground he wriggled through the bushes for a long distance along the bank. Reaching the plain, he made a dash for home. His face and arms were scratched and bleeding, and when he told his sister what had happened, she was grieved to think that she had made the snare which had brought so much sorrow to the innocent dormouse.

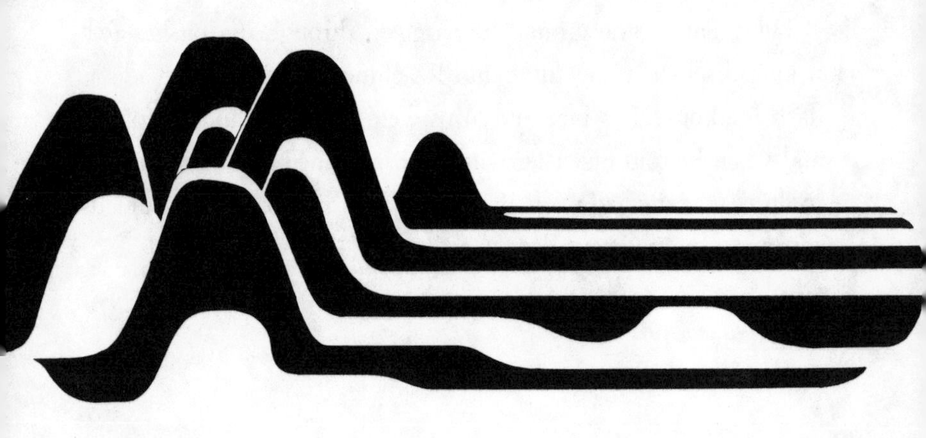

The Windmaker

ONCE there was a tribe of Indians who had always lived in the mountains. Their village was built at the foot of a very large mountain, and their lodges were made from branches of the pine-trees, covered with the skins of animals.

One day one of their hunters followed a bear's track for many miles. By evening he found himself a great distance from the village. He noticed that the hills around him were much smaller than those he had left, so he made up his mind to continue in the direction he had been going, which was eastwards, to see if the hills would grow smaller as he went. He rested during the night, and when the sun rose next morning, he continued walking towards the east. For several days he travelled, and at last he found himself on the edge of a very large plain. Miles and miles of green prairie lay before him, and he wondered what was beyond, on the other side of this vast plain.

He travelled back joyfully to the village and told the others of the tribe what he had discovered. As they listened they became anxious to see this great prairie and what lay beyond it. So they went to their chief and begged him to let them all go and travel until they should reach the other side of the prairie. The chief told them that this was a wrong thing to ask, because they were mountain Indians and so would never be happy away from the mountains. Still they begged and coaxed, and at length he said:

"I shall grant your request, my children, because my greatest wish is to see you happy. To-morrow we shall all make ready for our journey to this great prairie. I shall go with you, although it grieves me very much to leave my mountains, but your wish shall be granted."

By evening the next day the tribe was ready for the journey. They had taken down their lodges, and the branches of the pine-trees and the skins of the animals were packed on the mountain ponies. The chief rode in front on a small, white pony. His face looked very sad as they set out.

For many days they travelled, and at length they reached the edge of the prairie, as the hunter before them had done. They were all much astonished to see the great plain of green grass, and they told their chief that this land was much more beautiful than their mountains. He did not make them any reply. For several days they travelled across the prairie in the daytime and camped at night. Each morning they said as they prepared to move forward, "To-day we shall surely reach the other side of this prairie."

Each night, however, found them with as many miles in front of them as there were behind them. At last they grew weary, and began to wonder how long they would have to travel before they could see what was beyond this prairie. They had made their camp for the night on the bank of a river. This river was too wide and deep for them to cross, and they did not know what they would do. During the night a strange thing happened. Their lodges were caught as if by unseen hands, lifted high in the air, and tossed into the river. The little children clung to their mothers in terror, while these unseen hands seemed trying to pull them away and toss them after the lodges. The Indians, terrified, gathered around their chief.

"What is this?" they cried. "What is this awful thing that has such strength and which we cannot see?"

"It is the wind, my children," said the chief. "Far up on the mountain lives the Windmaker. This is his message to us, to tell us that he is angry, because we have left our mountain home. Let us all go back to our home and be happy once more."

But the Indians murmured at this. They did not wish to go back to the mountains. They wished to see what was beyond the great prairie. The chief sadly shook his head and said, "Well, my children, you must suffer what the Windmaker sends us."

Then up spoke a young warrior named Broken Arrow. He had long wished for a chance to show the chief that he was brave, for he loved the chief's daughter and knew he could not wed her until he had proven his bravery.

"Oh, chief," he said, "let me go to this Windmaker. Let me shoot my sharpest arrows at him, so that I may kill this wicked one who is causing so much sorrow."

The chief smiled at the brave youth and said, "My son, you may go, but it is a useless quest. This Windmaker cannot be killed."

Broken Arrow replied proudly, "We shall see. My arrows carry far and fly straight. This Windmaker shall feel their point."

The women of the tribe put food in a bag and several pairs of moccasins, and the young warrior set out on his journey. Day and night he travelled, and at last, after his food was all gone and his last pair of moccasins was nearly worn out, he reached the foot of the great mountain where the Windmaker lived. Looking up, he saw the monster, — a great, grey creature that seemed a part of the mountain itself. His head was crowned with snow-white hair that lay around his shoulders like drifts of snow. His huge ears stood out from the sides of his head, and as he waved them, a breeze came down the mountain side that almost took the warrior off his feet. Fitting an arrow into his bow, he let it fly. It was aimed for the Windmaker's heart, and was going straight there, when the monster moved one ear and the arrow flew to one side. The same fate overtook the next arrow, and the next. Still the warrior shot bravely on, but as each one came near the monster he waved his ears and blew it aside. At last every arrow had been spent, and the Windmaker was uninjured. There was nothing for the young warrior to do but to go back and tell of his failure. Sadly he turned away, and after many days' travelling he arrived at the camp, faint with hunger, and with bare and bleeding feet.

The chief smiled proudly as he saw him. "Welcome, my son," he said. "Do not feel sad. You have done nobly, and have proven to me how great a warrior you are. You shall be my son, and I am proud to call you that."

After the wedding feast that night, the chief told the Indians that on the morrow he was going to the mountain to see if he could kill the Windmaker. When they heard this, there was great weeping, and they begged him not to go. But he was firm, so they said, "Then we shall go with you. Where our chief goes, we go too, and we shall watch you fight this wicked one."

So, after many days' travelling, they all reached the foot of the great mountain where the Windmaker lived. Looking up, they could see him just as Broken Arrow had told them they would. The chief turned to them and said, "My children, you must remain here at the foot of this mountain, while I climb up to the top. There is no use in trying to shoot this great monster, for he will but blow my arrows away, so I must climb up and strike him with my tomahawk."

Again they begged him not to go, but again he was firm, and they sadly watched him begin to climb up the rocky side of the mountain. Little by little, he ascended the steep, rough hill, until at last he was almost at the feet of the Windmaker. All this time the monster had been perfectly still. Then suddenly, just as the chief was within reach of him, he waved both his ears, and a terrible gale tore down the mountain side, carrying rocks and stones with it. It caught the chief, lifted him off his feet and carried him down. When he reached the bottom he lay as if insensible for a few moments. Then, recovering his breath, he began to climb again. Once more the Windmaker let him nearly reach his feet before he made a movement. This time he sent a current of air against a large boulder resting on a narrow ledge. The chief leaped just in time, for it fell with a terrible noise on the very spot where he had stood.

Angered by this, the chief grasped his tomahawk more firmly, and dashing up a few paces, aimed a blow at the monster's feet.

But before it fell, the Windmaker waved both ears again. With a roar like thunder the gale swept down, carrying the brave chief with it. It tossed him in the air, turned him around two or three times, and hurled him into a clump of fir-trees at the foot of the mountain. The Indians ran frantically to the spot and picked him up, but he was quite dead. They buried him sadly where he had fallen, at the foot of the tender firs. Then they went quietly back to their village in the mountains and have been content to live there ever since.

Moowis

In a certain tribe in the far West there was a maiden who was very beautiful. Many warriors loved her, but she would listen to none of them.

In the same tribe there was a young man who was called Beau-man, because he was so beautifully dressed. He was very hand-some too, and so when he fell in love with the maiden, he felt sure she would love him also; but when he came to see her, she would not listen, and when he tried to make her hear, she made a motion with her hand which means contempt. This made him feel very mean. All his friends laughed at him, and this made him so very angry that he went away to his tent and lay down. He remained without eating anything for many weeks. His parents and friends all coaxed him to get up, but he would not.

At length the time came for the tribe to move camp, as this was just a hunting trip, and when the summer arrived they always went back to the village. They asked Beau-man to come with them, but still he would not move. So they lifted the tent, and left him lying there in his bed all alone.

The next day he got up, for he had thought of a splendid plan to have revenge on the maiden. He knew a spirit who would help him when asked.

He began to gather all the bits of colored cloth, old beads, and feathers that were lying on the ground where the camp had been. Most of them were very dirty, and some were wet with snow. But he put them all in one pile, and then with the help of the spirit, he made them all look clean. Then he made beaded moccasins from some of the scraps; leggings and a coat from some others. At last a frontlet with feathers sticking in it for the head. He gathered up snow and dirt, and filled the moccasins and the rest of the suit with it. The spirit changed the whole thing into a man, — a fine-looking warrior, to whom was given the name Moowis. The Beau-man at once took him to the village where the maiden lived.

Moowis was kindly received by the chief, who invited him into his lodge. He was finely dressed, and held himself so proudly that the maiden fell in love with him. The chief asked him to sit near the fire. But he could not sit there very long, as the heat began to melt the snow, and soon he would have been a pile of rags. He put a boy between himself and the fire, and kept moving away until he was near the door.

Then the chief came and asked him to sit in the bridegroom's chair. This meant that he was married to the maiden. When it became evening, Moowis said he must go now, as he had a long journey to make. The maiden begged to go with him, but he told her she could not. Still she coaxed so hard that he asked the Beau-man what he should do. "Let her go with you," he answered; "it will serve her right."

In a little while they set out. Moowis walked so fast that the maiden had to run to keep up, and in a short time she was very tired. Still he walked on so swiftly that he was soon far ahead. They walked all night, and when the sun rose the bridegroom was almost out of sight. As the day grew warm, his snow began to melt, and as it did so, his fine clothes began to turn back into rags. Then they began to fall off. First the maiden found his mit-tens, next his moccasins, then she picked up his coat. She walked on calling, "Moowis, where are you?" But all she could find was bits of rags, beads, and feathers scattered over the fields. She wandered on from one village to another calling, "Moowis, Moowis, oh, Moowis, where have you gone?"

The village maidens turned her cry into a song, and used to chant it as she passed. She never saw anything more of him, although she wandered on for years, always calling, "Moowis."

The Daughters of the Star

THERE once lived, in a deep forest, a hunter named Waupee, or the White Hawk. Every day he returned from the chase with birds and animals which he had killed, for he was very skilful.

One day he walked through the forest till at last he reached the edge of it, and there before him lay the wide prairie. The grass was so soft and green, and there were so many flowers, that he wandered on for a while. He could see that no one lived there, as no trace of footsteps was to be seen. Suddenly he came to a circle on the prairie. It looked as if people had run around in a ring until the grass was trampled down. As he could see no marks of footsteps leading away from the ring, he wondered very much whose feet could have marked out the circle. Then he made up his mind to hide, so that he might see if any one came.

After a while, he heard the sound of beautiful music. It seemed to come from the sky. As he looked up he saw something coming down through the air, and the music sounded like the singing of girls. As the object came closer, he saw that it was a wicker basket, and in it were twelve beautiful maidens. When the basket reached the ground, they all jumped out and began to dance around the circle. They were all very beautiful, but Waupee picked out the youngest as the one he liked best. He watched them as long as he could, then ran out to clasp the youngest in his arms. But as soon as the maidens saw the figure of a man, they ran to the basket, jumped in, and were at once drawn up to the sky.

Waupee was left alone on the prairie, and he felt very sad to think he had frightened away the beautiful maidens. He went back slowly to his lodge, but could not rest all night. The next day he came again to the magic circle.

This time he changed himself into an opossum. He had not waited long when the wicker basket again floated down. The sisters jumped out and began the same dance. Waupee crept towards them; but when they saw him, they at once ran to the basket and climbed in. It began to ascend, but stopped when a short distance up.

"Perhaps," said the oldest sister, "he has come to show us the way the mortals dance."

"Oh, no!" said the youngest: "let us go up quickly."

They all began to sing their sweet song, and the basket rose out of sight.

Again Waupee was sad, but he made up his mind that the next day he would act more wisely. So, when he came back, he found the stump of a tree where a family of mice lived. He moved the stump over near the circle and changed himself into one of the mice. Again the sisters came, and began their dance.

"Look," said the youngest sister, "that stump was not there before." But the other sisters laughed at her and ran over to it. Then out came all the mice, Waupee among them. The sisters began to chase and kill the mice, and at last only one was left alive. The youngest sister ran after it, and was just about to hit it, when it changed into Waupee. He clasped her in his arms, while the other sisters sprang for the basket and were drawn up to the sky.

The maiden wept at being left alone, but Waupee wiped away her tears and took her home to his little lodge. He was very good to her and at last she grew very happy. But a few years afterwards, when her little son was able to walk, she took him to the magic ring. She felt very lonely when she thought of her sisters and of her father, the Star. So she made up her mind to go back to them. She made a basket of reeds, and putting her little son in it, she seated herself and began to sing the old chant. The basket at once rose in the air and floated out of sight.

When Waupee was coming home, he heard this sweet song. He knew it was one the sisters used to sing, so he ran at once to the magic circle, but the basket had almost disappeared. He called and called, but no answer came down to him, and at last it was gone.

He threw himself down on the ground and wept. Then, when night came, he rose and went home to his empty lodge.

As the years went on the maiden was very happy in her old home, but the son wished to go and see his birthplace. The grandfather heard him, and said to the maiden, "Go down to the earth and show your son his birthplace, and when you are coming back, bring your husband with you. But when he comes, tell him to bring a part of each kind of bird and animal he has killed."

This the maiden did. Waupee was delighted to have them return, and at once set to work to hunt and kill one of every kind of bird and animal. It took him many days to do this, but at last all were gathered. He took a claw of some birds, a wing of others, a tail of some animals, and the feet of others. Then they all stepped into the basket and it took them up to the sky.

The Star grandfather was so pleased with Waupee's gift, that he called all his people to a feast. After it was over, he told them to choose what they liked best from the earthly things. Some chose a wing, others a paw, and so on, and as they did so they were at once changed into an animal or bird like the one they had chosen.

Waupee was pleased with this idea and chose the feather of a white hawk. His wife and son chose the same, and all were changed into these graceful birds. They slowly spread out their white wings and floated away towards the earth.

Passing through the clouds they found themselves above the snow-capped mountains. They flew on, until at length they saw the green tops of trees far below them. In great circles they began to descend, and in a few minutes alighted in the topmost branches of a tall tree.

Waupee then spoke: "We shall build our nest in this tree, and into it we shall weave parts of our old lodge, where we lived so happily together. Let us go now and gather these; then we shall begin our nest."

Koto and the Bird

ONCE there was a little Cree boy named Koto. His father was a chief and a great hunter, and Koto always longed for the time when he would be able to hunt like his father and bring back large game to the wigwam. One summer day the chief and all the hunters were away on a hunting trip. There was no one left in the camp but a few of the women and some children. Koto wandered around, not knowing what to do, when suddenly he thought of a very daring thing. One pony had been left because it had been lame, and now Koto made up his mind that he would get on its back and gallop over the prairie. He knew that the pony's foot was nearly better, and he thought that one gallop could not hurt it.

So he jumped on the pony's back, waved his arms, and called

out to it to run, and away they went. Koto's long, dark hair and the pony's mane blew in the wind, and they both were enjoying the gallop when something terrible happened. The pony caught his foot in a badger hole and fell heavily to the ground. Koto was tossed in the air, and then fell with one foot pinned under him.

For a long time the two sufferers lay there in the hot sun on the prairie. At length Koto's mother, who had missed him, found them. She carried Koto back to the wigwam and laid him on his bed of skins. She told him that his leg was broken and that the pony's leg was broken also, and that the hunters would have to kill it when they returned. Poor Koto wept bitterly. He did not mind his own broken leg, but to think that he had really killed the little pony nearly broke his heart. For many days he lay on his bed, and at last he was able to get up and move around with the help of a little crutch, which his father had made from the branch of a tree.

When winter came, the Indians moved their camp to the woods along the bank of the Assiniboine River. Koto was not able to walk well, so remained in his lodge until all the camp had been moved. Then his father came to carry him to the camp that was protected from the cold north wind.

"My son," he said, as he walked along with Koto in his arms, "I have a surprise for you. You shall not live in a wigwam this winter."

"Why not?" asked Koto. "I like my wigwam. It is warm and keeps the cold wind away."

"Wait, and you shall see," said his father. "You will like your new lodge much better."

When they reached the camp, Koto saw what the chief had

meant. During the summer some white men had camped there and had built a log cabin for themselves. Then they had gone away, leaving the little cabin deserted, and now the chief had taken it for his lodge. Koto was very much pleased with his new home, and the door which opened on hinges was always a great surprise to him. He was not able to go out during that long winter, but he was never lonely, for the first day they were in the cabin a strange visitor came. It was a little, brown bird which had been deserted by its mate, and it flew in to get away from the cold. All winter it remained with Koto, feeding from his food at mealtime, and hopping around him during the day as he was weaving his baskets. At night it slept on a little board that was nailed to the wall near Koto's bed of skins.

When springtime came and the door was left open, Koto noticed that the bird's mate had returned. It flew to the bushes near the house and called to Koto's bird, but she would not go, and at last her mate came to the doorway. Again he called, and this time she went out, but she came back at mealtime and remained with Koto all night. Every day after that she would fly out in the morning and come back three or four times during the day, while her mate would never come past the doorway. Then one day she did not come back. Koto watched and waited for her. The long day passed and evening came, still there was no sign of the bird. The next day went by, and the next, and little Koto began to look very sad as he sat at the door watching for her.

At last he hobbled out and sat very quietly under the trees. In a little while he came back as quickly as he could, his face shining for joy. When he entered the cabin, he looked around eagerly. Then his face grew sad again.

"She is not here," he said sadly. "My little bird is not here."

"No, she is not here," said his mother. "Did you think she was?"

"Yes, I saw her fly in, but she is not here."

Koto went out again and seated himself under the trees once more, but he saw no sign of his bird all the rest of that day. The next day he went to the same place to watch, and not long after he came hobbling in eagerly with his face shining for joy as before. He looked around the cabin, and again he grew sad, for there was no bird to be seen.

Each day after that the same thing happened. As he sat under the trees he saw the little bird fly into the cabin, but when he entered there was no bird to be seen. He grew sadder and looked so thin that the chief became sad, too.

"My son," he said, "you must not think of this bird. It has flown away. It will not come back. This is a spirit bird that you see enter the cabin. Try not to think of it and be happy."

But the little Cree boy only shook his head and said, "I saw her go in and she does not come out and she is not in the cabin. Where is she? Where is my little bird?"

So the chief made up his mind that he would watch and see if the little bird really did fly into the cabin. The next day he watched with Koto under the trees, and in a few minutes the little boy grasped his hand.

"Look," he said, "look, there is my little bird." And there in a tree near them were two brown birds, one of them Koto's pet. They flew away together; then one, when it reached the side of the cabin, suddenly disappeared. Quickly seizing his father's hand, Koto and the chief reached the door of the little home. They looked eagerly around the room, but there was not a bird to be seen. They searched every place, for the chief was sure that he had seen it enter. There was no trace of it any place. Going out, he looked at the side of the little house, and there was a hole between the logs where the bird might easily enter. Coming in, he looked for the hole on the inside, but could not find it. Then he noticed that an old, grey jacket, which had been left there by the white men, was hanging where the hole ought to be.

He took down the jacket and Koto gave a cry of delight. For from a pocket of the coat peaked the head of his little bird, and there was the hole between the logs where the coat had hung. The bird seemed quite pleased that they had found her, and after a while flew off her nest to peck from Koto's hand. After some days her eggs were hatched, and then the father bird consented to enter the cabin and help feed the young ones. When the little birds grew large enough, they flew away with the father bird, but for the rest of the summer Koto's little brown friend remained with him, watching him weave his baskets, and seemed very pleased when at last he was able to walk a little.

When fall came, she went away with the other birds, but this time Koto was not sad, for he knew she was happy, and he was happy, too, because he could now walk.

The Humpbacked Manitou

BOKWEWA and his brother lived in a lodge in the forest, far away from the rest of the world. They were both Manitous and could do many wonderful things. Bokwewa had the most gifts and knew all the secrets of the woods, but his body was deformed. The brother was very handsome. His body was very straight, and he could run and do many things that Bokwewa could not do. But he was not as wise as the humpbacked Manitou. Bokwewa used to tell his brother how to hunt and shoot and fish. Then the brother would go and get the food, and bring it back to the lodge. Bokwewa did not go out very much, of course.

One day the brother said, "Bokwewa, I am tired of living so quietly. Where are all the rest of the people? I am going away to find them and to get a wife."

Bokwewa tried to coax him not to go, but the brother was determined. He made ready for his journey, and departed. In a few days he returned, bringing a beautiful maiden with him. Bokwewa was very kind to his brother's wife and she was good to him, so they became great friends. One day the brother was away hunting. Bokwewa was sitting by one side of the fire in the lodge; the wife was sitting on the other side. Suddenly the door was opened, and a strong, tall man entered. He seized the maiden and began to pull her to the door. She screamed, and tried to get away from him; but he held her fast. Bokwewa pulled and fought with all his strength. The tall man pushed him against the door and hurt his back. Then he dashed out with the maiden, and took her away with him.

When the brother returned, he found Bokwewa weeping with sorrow; and when he heard what had happened, he wept also. Bokwewa tried to comfort him, but the brother only lay on the bed, refusing to eat anything, and weeping bitterly. For several days he stayed there. At length he arose and said, "Bokwewa, I am going to the village where that mighty Manitou lives. He has stolen my wife."

"Oh, do not go," said Bokwewa, "for that village is many miles to the south. The people who live there are idle and know only of pleasure. They have many snares set by the roadside to catch you. Do not try to go amongst them, for you will become like them and think only of pleasure."

"I am not afraid of anything," said the brother. "I must go."

"Well, then," said Bokwewa, "I shall tell you of two dangers that lie in the path. When you first start, you will find a grape-vine across your path. Do not eat any of its fruit, for it is poisonous. It will make you become very careless. Then, farther on you will come across something that looks like bear's fat. It is clear, like jelly. Do not eat of it, for it is frogs' eggs and will make you forget your home."

The brother promised to remember these warnings, and set out for the village.

He had not gone very far when he noticed a grape-vine lying across the road. The grapes were beautiful and juicy, so he ate some. Some distance on he came to a jellylike mass, and he ate it. This was the frogs' eggs, and he at once forgot his home and brother, and even his wife. He travelled on for two days, and towards evening came in sight of the large village. The people in it seemed to be having a good time. Some were dancing and singing, and many of the women were beating corn in golden dishes. When they saw him coming, they ran out, shouting, "Here comes Bokwewa's brother to visit us."

They welcomed him with joy, and led him into the village. In a short time he was beating corn with the women. That is the surest sign to the Indians that a warrior has lost his bravery.

Days and weeks went by, and still he did not try to find his wife, although she was living in that same village. Bokwewa waited at home, hoping each day that his brother would return. At length, when some years had gone by, he set out to find him. As he travelled along the same road, he passed the grape-vine and the frogs' eggs. But they held no danger for him, as he did not taste them. When he came in sight of the village, he felt sorry for the people, who were wasting their lives in idle games and other pleasures. As he came closer, the people ran out, shouting, "Oh, Bokwewa has come to visit us! The good Bokwewa of whom we have heard so much! Welcome to our village!"

Bokwewa entered with them and found his brother. He was still beating corn with the women, and seemed very happy. Bokwewa coaxed him to come home, but he would not listen. He seemed content to stay there and do no work. This made Bokwewa very sorry, for he knew his brother was no longer a brave warrior. When evening came Bokwewa went down to the riverside. There he changed himself into one of those hair snakes sometimes seen in running water. After a while, the wife came down with a pitcher to get some water.

"Pick me up," said the hair snake, "and leave me in your pitcher."

The wife did as she was told, and took the pitcher to her lodge.

That night the Manitou who had stolen her wanted a drink. In the dark he did not see the hair snake in the water, so drank it. In a few minutes he was dead. Then Bokwewa returned to his former shape. He went again to his brother and tried to make him come home. But the brother refused. Bokwewa told him that these pleasures would not last forever, and his tears fell as he saw that his brother would not come. So he said good-bye to him and disappeared.

After Bokwewa had gone, the brother seemed to remember parts of his past life. He looked around and saw his wife at a little distance. At once he remembered everything, and going to her, he wept and begged her to forgive him and his neglect. She kissed him fondly, and then hand in hand they walked away from the treacherous land of pleasure, back to the lodge where Bokwewa waited for them.

The Tribe that grew out of a Shell

ONCE, when the land along the Missouri River was uninhabited, save by the beaver and other animals, a snail lay asleep on the bank of the river. One day the waters began to rise, and soon came up to where he lay. They swept him out, and he was carried some miles down by the current. When the waves lowered, he found himself bedded deep in the mud. He tried to free himself, but he could not. He was hungry and tired, and at last became so discouraged that he would not try any more.

Then a strange thing happened. He felt his shell crack, and his head began to rise upright. His body and legs grew and lengthened, and at last he felt arms stretching out from his sides. Then he stood upright — a MAN.

He felt very stupid at first, but after a while some thoughts came to him. He knew he was hungry and wished he were a snail again; for he knew how to get food as a snail, but not as a man. He saw plenty of birds, but did not know how to kill them. He wandered on through the forest, until he became so tired that he lay down to rest.

He heard a gentle voice speaking to him, and looking up, he saw the Great Spirit, who was seated on a snow-white horse. His eyes shone like stars, and his hair like threads of gold.

"Wasbashas, why are you trembling?"

"I am frightened," replied the man, "because I stand before the One who raised me from the ground. I am faint from hunger, for I have eaten nothing since I left the shell in the bank of the river."

"Look, Wasbashas," said the spirit, as he drew forth a beautiful bow and arrow. Putting an arrow into the bow, he aimed at a bird in a tree near by. He shot, and the bird fell. A deer passed just then, and the spirit shot it, also.

"Now, Wasbashas," said the spirit, "I shall show you how to skin this deer, and show you how to make a blanket. Then you must learn to cook the flesh. I shall give you the gift of fire. For now that you are a man, you must not eat raw food. You shall be placed at the head of all the animals and birds."

After the spirit had shown him the things he had promised, both horse and rider arose in the air and vanished.

Wasbashas walked on down the river until he came to a place where a beaver was lying.

"Good-day," said the beaver. "Who are you?"

"I am a man. The Great Spirit raised me from a shell, and now I am head of all the animals. And who are you?"

"I am a beaver. Will you come with me until I show you how we build our lodges?"

Wasbashas followed the beaver and watched him cut down a tree with his teeth. Then the animal showed him how they dammed up the river, by letting the trees fall across it and filling the spaces between with mud and leaves.

"Now will you come and visit my lodge?" said the beaver chief. He led Wasbashas to his neat lodge made of clay and shaped like a cone. The floor was carpeted with mats. The beaver's wife and daughter received the stranger kindly. They busied themselves getting a meal ready, and soon brought dishes of peeled poplar and alder bark. Wasbashas did not like the taste of it, but managed to eat a few pieces. The beavers seemed to enjoy the meal very much.

Wasbashas had been watching the daughter, and he liked her nice, tidy ways and the respect she showed her father. In the evening he asked the chief if he would give the maiden to him for his bride. The chief was very pleased at the idea, for he liked Wasbashas.

The beaver invited all the animals to the feast, which was to be held the next day. Early the following morning they began to arrive. First came the beavers, each bringing a present of a lump of clay on his flat tail. Next came the otters, each bringing a large fish in his mouth. Later in the morning came the minks, the water-rats, and the weasels, all very proud to accept the invitation of the great chief of the beavers.

When the animals had all assembled, the beavers held a council among themselves. After talking for some time they invited the other animals to follow them. And going a short distance down the river bank, they stopped. Each beaver took the lump of clay he had brought with him and placed it near the water's edge. Then they began to build a dome-shaped lodge of small pieces of trees and the clay. After several hours of steady work it was finished, and then they went to the chief's lodge, where the feast was to be held.

When the meal was over the snail man and the beaver maiden were led to their lodge, which was the wedding-gift of the beavers. Here they lived happy ever after. Many years later their descendants were called the Osages tribe of Indians.

The Story of the Indian Corn

SOME years ago the Ottawa Indians inhabited the Manatoline Islands. Their enemies were the Iroquois Indians, who lived on the lake shore near the islands. One night they came and attacked the Ottawas. The two tribes fought for a long time, but at last the Iroquois won, and the Ottawas were driven away from their islands. They wandered off towards the Mississippi River, where they settled near a small lake, many miles away from their home.

The Manatoline Islands were now uninhabited, except by an Indian magician, whose name was Masswaweinini. He remained behind to act as sentry for his tribe. He guarded the beautiful islands and kept a close watch on their enemy, the Iroquois. Two young boys stayed with him to paddle his canoe. In the daytime they used to paddle close to the shore, so that the Iroquois could not see them, and at night they slept in the deep woods.

One morning Masswaweinini rose early and left the two boys asleep. He walked a long distance through the woods, hunting for game. At last he found himself on the edge of a wide prairie. He began to walk across it, when a man suddenly appeared in front of him. He was very tiny and had some red feathers in his hair. "Good-morning, Masswaweinini," he said. "You are a very strong man, are you not?"

"Yes," replied the magician. "I am as strong as any man, but no stronger."

The tiny man then pulled out his tobacco-pouch and pipe.

"Come and smoke with me," he said, "and then we must have a wrestling match. If you can throw me, you must say, 'I have thrown Wagemena.' "

So they smoked together, but when the little man was ready to wrestle, the magician did not like to do it, for he was afraid he might hurt the tiny fellow. But the other insisted, and so they began to wrestle. The magician soon found that the little man was very strong and quick, and he felt himself growing weaker every moment. But at last he succeeded in tripping the man with the red feathers, and he fell. Then the magician said, "I have thrown you, Wagemena." At once the little man vanished, and in his place lay an ear of corn, with a red tassel where the feathers had been. As he stood staring at it the corn spoke. "Pick me up," it said, "and pull off my outer covering. Then take off my kernels and scatter them over the ground. Break my cob into three parts and throw them near the trees. Depart, but come back after one moon, and see what has happened."

The magician did exactly as the corn had told him, and went away. At the end of the time he came back. To his surprise, he found green blades of corn coming through the ground where the kernels had been scattered. And near the trees pumpkin-vines were growing where the cobs of the corn had been thrown.

He had not told the young boys of his adventure with the tiny man, so he did not tell them anything of the growing corn. All the rest of that summer he busied himself in closely watching the Iroquois, who were still prowling near the islands. Very often he killed a deer, and the boys would cook the meat over their camp-fire. One day, when the summer was nearly over, he paddled his canoe around the island till he came near the wrestling ground. He stepped ashore, and left the two boys to watch the canoe, while he walked to the field. To his great astonishment, he found the corn in full ear, and the pumpkins of an immense size. He pulled some ripened ears of corn and gathered some pumpkins. Then a voice spoke to him from the corn. "You have conquered me, Masswaweinini," it said. "If you had not done so, you would have been killed yourself. But your strength made you win the victory, and now you shall always have my body for food. It will be nourishment for you and your tribe."

Thus the Ottawa Indians were given the gift of the maize; and to this day their descendants are noted for the care that they take of their immense fields of corn.

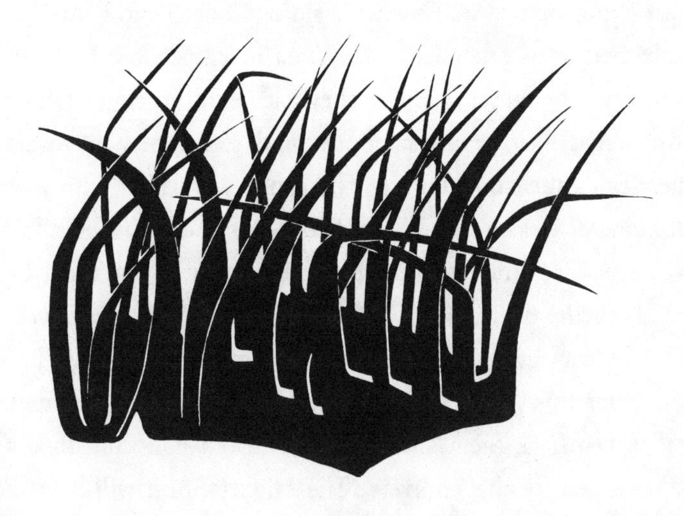

The Magician of Lake Huron

THE Manatoline, or Spirit, Islands were supposed to be a favorite abode of the Manitous, or spirits. Perhaps that is why many strange things happened there. One night, as Masswaweinini, the magician, was lying asleep, a sound of voices wakened him. "This is Masswaweinini," said the first voice; "we must have his heart."

"How shall we get it?" said the second voice.

"I shall put my hand into his mouth," said the first, "and pull it out that way."

The magician felt a hand being slipped between his teeth. He waited until the fingers were all in his mouth, then he bit them hard and they came off. He heard a cry, then the strangers disappeared. In the morning he arose, but could find no trace of any one. But when he came down to the water's edge, he saw a canoe with two people in it. They were sitting at each end of the canoe, with their arms stretched out. When he came close to them, he saw they were fairies, and that they had been turned to stone. One of them had lost the fingers of one hand, so he knew they were his enemies of the night before. The canoe was laden with bags of all kinds of treasures, and it was the most beautiful boat he had ever seen. He lifted out the stone figures and put them in the woods. As he turned away, one of the figures spoke to him.

"Masswaweinini," it said, "the canoes of the Ottawa Indians will, after this, always be well laden like our canoe. Your tribe was driven from their land by their cruel enemies, but they shall be rewarded for their bravery. The Mighty Spirit will help them, and they shall be given many treasures in their new home."

The magician then went back to the boat and lifted out the bags. He carried the boat and hid it among the trees. When he opened the bags, he found meat and fish and many other things, and took them to his camp.

As he rested in his lodge that night, he would have been very happy, if he had not been so sorry for his old father and mother. He thought of them many miles away with none of the comforts he had. "I shall go and bring them," he said. He had only to think of going when at once he could move like the wind. So before morning he found himself at the poor, little camp of his parents. They were still asleep, so without making any noise, he took them in his arms and carried them back to his lodge. When they awakened in the morning, they were delighted to find themselves with their son. All day long they wandered through the fields and by the shore, and were as happy as children. As the days and weeks went by, they seemed to grow happier still. But one night the magician saw his old father look in his tobacco-pouch and then sigh.

"I know what it is you want, my father, it is tobacco; you have not had any for many moons. Now I shall get some."

"How can you do that?" asked the father, in surprise. "You are surrounded by enemies and cut off from all supplies."

"I shall make my enemies give me some," said the magician.

That night he set out on a long journey across the frozen lake. So swiftly did he travel, that by morning he had reached the village of his enemies. They were surprised to see him, but invited him into their lodges. "I thank you," he said, "but I shall not go into any lodge. I shall build a fire on the shore of the lake."

He made himself a tent with the branches of trees, built a fire, and sat beside it.

"Why have you come to visit us?" asked the chief.

"I want some tobacco for my father," replied the magician.

"Is that all?" said the Indian. "You shall have it;" and he opened his tobacco-pouch and gave some tobacco to Masswaweinini. The other Indians did the same, so now the magician had a large supply to take home. When it became dark, he lay down to sleep beside his fire. In the middle of the night, the chief and some Indians rushed in, shouting, "You are a dead man."

"No, I am not," said the magician, "but you are." With his tomahawk he hit left and right. In a few minutes six lay dead beside him. Then he wrapped his blanket around him, gathered up his tobacco, and set off. By evening he had reached his father's lodge, and spread out his gift before him. The old man was delighted with the present, and thanked him many times for his kindness. When spring came, the magician built a beautiful lodge for his parents on the edge of the wrestling ground, and all through the summer they watched the corn and pumpkins grow.

The Fairies' Cliff

AN Indian chief once had ten daughters. They were all very beautiful, especially the youngest. When they grew to be women, nine of them married handsome, young warriors. But the youngest maiden would not listen to any of the young men who came to see her at her father's lodge. After a while, she married an old man with grey hair, and so feeble that he could hardly walk. Her father and sisters were very angry, but she would not listen to them. She said only, "I am very happy, and so nothing else matters."

One evening, the father asked his ten daughters and their husbands to come to his lodge for a feast. On the way there, the nine sisters kept saying, as they looked at the youngest maiden and her husband: "Our poor sister, is it not a pity she is married to such an old man? See, he can hardly walk. Would it not be a good thing if he were to fall and kill himself?"

As they were saying this, they noticed that the old man kept looking up at the Evening Star, and every once in a while he would utter a low call.

"See," said one of the sisters, "he thinks the Evening Star is his father and is calling to him."

Just then, they were passing a hollow log which lay by the roadside. When the old man noticed it, he suddenly dropped on his hands and knees and crawled in at one end. When he came out at the other end, he was no longer an old man; he had been changed into a tall, handsome, young chief. But his wife was no longer a beautiful maiden. She had been changed into a bent, old woman, hobbling along with a stick. The young husband was very kind to her and took good care of her all the rest of the way to the father's lodge. He seemed very sorry that she had been changed like this, but he loved her just the same as before. During the feast the young husband heard a voice speak to him. It seemed to come from the skies. Looking up, he saw the Evening Star shining in through a crack in the roof.

"My son," the Star said to him, "many years ago an evil spirit changed you into an old man, but that spirit has now lost its power. You are free, and may come home and live with me. Your wife shall be beautiful once more, and you shall have everything you can wish for."

The others had not heard this voice, so they were very much surprised when they felt the lodge begin to rise in the air. As it floated upwards, the bark changed into beautiful silver gauze. It was now a lodge made of wings of insects. The young chief looked at his wife and saw that she was a beautiful maiden once more.

Her dress was changed into one of shining, green silk, and her stick became a silver feather. The sisters and their husbands had been changed into birds with bright-colored feathers. Some were parrots, some blue jays, some singing birds that flew around and sang their sweet songs. At the side of the lodge was a large cage for the birds. Upwards the lodge floated till they found themselves in the Evening Star. Everything was silvery white here and very peaceful. The Star was very glad to see his son.

"Hang up that cage of birds which you have brought with you by the lodge door, and then come and sit down while we talk."

The young chief did as he was told. He sat on one side of his father, while his wife sat on the other, and the Star father told them many stories.

"You must be careful," he said, "not to let the beams of the next star shine on you. That is the Evil Star which turned you into an old man. If it shines on you again, you might once more be changed, so be very careful."

The young chief promised to remember his father's warnings, and he always kept away from the Evil Star. They lived happily together for several years. Then one day their young son wanted to learn to hunt. He had heard that the people on the earth could shoot with bow and arrows, and he wished to learn. The Evening Star did not like to refuse his young grandson anything, so he made him a little bow and arrows. He showed him how to use them; then said, "I shall open the bird-cage and let out the birds. You may try to shoot them, if you like."

This delighted the young boy, and so for many days he tried to shoot a bird. His arrows always fell to one side. But he kept on trying, and one day the arrow sank deep in the breast of one of the birds. The boy was very proud, but what was his surprise, when he went to pick up the bird, to find that it had changed into a beautiful maiden with an arrow sticking in her breast. It was one of his aunts, who had been changed back into her earthly form. As her blood fell on the ground of this pure and spotless planet, the spell was broken.

The boy felt himself sinking down through the air. He fell slowly, as if he had wings. At last his feet touched the ground, and he found himself on a high, rocky island. He was delighted to see his aunts and uncles all following him. They floated down through the air until at last they too reached the rock. Then came the silvery lodge, with his father and mother, with its bark looking like the shining wings of insects. The lodge sank down until it reached the cliff, and there they all made their home. They had been given back their earthly bodies, but were only the size of fairies.

The top of the cliff, which had been bare before, now grew soft with green grass. In the grass, bright flowers blossomed, and tiny pools of water glistened here and there. The fairies were all very happy to have been given such a beautiful home, and, looking up, they thanked the Evening Star. His soft beams fell on them and they heard his gentle voice say, "Be happy, my children, until I call you again to your home in the sky. I shall keep watch over you until then." So from that time they have been very contented.

On calm summer evenings, they always come out on top of the rock to dance and sing. And when the moon is shining very brightly, you may see the silver lodge on the very highest part of the cliff; you may also, if you listen very hard, hear the voices of the happy little dancers.

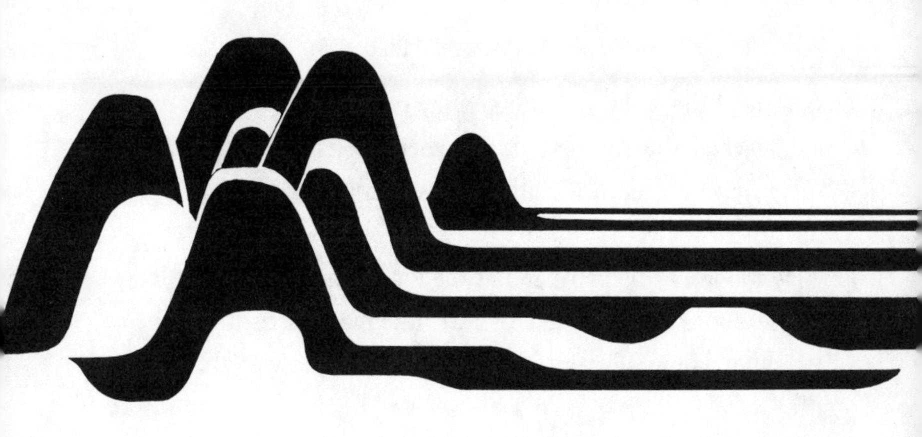

The Stone Canoe

ONCE a beautiful Chippewa maiden died on the day she was to have married a brave, young warrior. He was very brave, but this sorrow was almost too great for him to bear. He sat down at the door of his lodge and would not go hunting with the other Indians.

All that he could think of was the dead maiden, and he wished and wished that he might go to the Land of Souls, where he knew she now lived. But he did not know where this land was. All that the old people could tell him was that it lay to the south. So, after sorrowing for many days, he made up his mind to try to find it. He put some food in a bag, gathered up his arrows and bow, and calling his dog to him, started off. On he went for many days, and everything looked the same as in the land he had left — forests, hills, and valleys, with snow lying thick on the ground and matted in the trees. Then gradually the snow began to vanish, and as he went on he saw trees with leaves budding on them, and could hear the songs of birds. At the end of a few more days, he had reached the southern land, where all is warm and bright. There he saw a narrow path leading through a forest and up a hill.

He followed this path, and at the top of the hill found a lodge. At the door of the lodge stood an Indian, dressed in a robe of bearskins. He was a very old man, but his eyes were bright and soft.

"Come in, my grandson," he said. "I have been expecting you. The maiden whom you seek passed here a few days ago. You may follow her and enter the Land of Souls, but you must leave your body behind with me. My lodge is the gateway into that beautiful land, and you do not need your body there, nor your arrows, nor your bow. Leave them with me and I shall keep them safe for you. Look yonder! Do you see that deep gorge and the beautiful plain beyond? That is the Land of Souls, and the one you seek is already there."

Suddenly the young man felt himself grow very light, and his feet began to run as though they were winged. Everything looked the same to him, only more beautiful, and the little animals did not seem afraid. They seemed to know that he would not kill them. As he went on swiftly through the forest, he noticed that the trees did not stop him. He seemed to pass right through them, and he saw then that they were only images of trees.

A last he came to a beautiful lake, whose waters were clear and sparkling. In the centre of this lake was an island, with green grass and flowers and birds. Then, to his joy, he noticed a canoe tied to the shore of the lake. It was made of shining, white stone and had paddles that shone, also. He climbed in and pushed away from the shore, and, to his surprise, he saw the maiden whom he loved, in a canoe exactly like his, floating beside him. They kept close together and began to cross the lake. Its waves seemed to be rising, and at a distance looked ready to swallow them up. But when the huge waves drew close, they passed by and left them unharmed, and the maiden and her lover saw that they were only the shapes of waves. But another thing frightened them. It was *the clearness of the water,* for as they looked down, they could see the bodies of people who had been drowned. And in the water all along, there were men and women of all ages struggling and sinking in the waves. Only the canoes of the little children floated on in safety.

At last their canoes reached the shore of the island, and jumping out, they roamed joyfully over the soft grass. They felt that the very air was food, and thought only of great things. For there was nothing that was sad here in this land, no cold winds, no hunger — only brightness and joy.

As the warrior wandered by the maiden's side, he heard the voice of the Master of Life speaking to him. "Go back," he said, "to the land whence you came. Your work is not completed yet. Go back and be a good man, and do all the work that I send to you. You must leave the spirit whom you love, but she shall wait here for you, for she is accepted, and shall always remain young and happy. When your work is finished, I shall call you also from the land of hunger and tears, to come to this beautiful Land of Souls."

So the young man said farewell to the maiden, and getting into the canoe, he was carried across the lake. In a few minutes, he was at the lodge of the old man. The Indian smiled when he saw him.

"Enter, my grandson," he said, "and you will find your body within."

The young man obeyed, and when he came forth he felt as when he had first arrived. But his heart was brave now. The Indian smiled again at him.

"I see how brave and strong you are," he said, "and my message to you is: always remain cheerful and brighten every sad life that you see."

The young man promised to obey the message, and, with one long look at the Land of Souls, he turned and began his journey towards his home.

The White Feather

An old man and his grandson once lived together on an island. The little boy had no father, nor mother, nor brothers, nor sisters. They had all been killed by six giants, who lived many miles away. The little boy had never seen any person but his grandfather. They lived very happily together. The old man loved the boy and was kind to him. As the little fellow grew tall and strong, the old man taught him how to hunt, so that by the time he was a young man he was a good hunter.

One day when he was walking in the woods, he heard a voice calling to him. He turned in surprise, for he had never heard any one but his grandfather speak. He could see no one, but again he heard the voice. It was saying, "You will some day be the wearer of the White Feather."

He looked all around him, and then noticed something that he had taken for a withered tree. It was a man who was made of wood from his breast down to his feet. He seemed to be very old, and was fastened to the ground. When he saw the young man was looking at him, he said, "Come here, I wish to tell you something. There was an old belief in your tribe that some day a boy would grow up to be a very great warrior. He was to wear a white feather as a sign of his bravery and great skill. You are that boy. When you go home, you will find there a white feather, a pipe, and a tobacco-pouch. Put the white feather in your hair. Then smoke the pipe, and you will find that the smoke will turn into pigeons. This is another sign that you will be wise and good."

The old man ceased speaking, and the young grandson returned home to his lodge. He found the feather and the pipe both lying there. He did as the old man told him, and when he smoked, blue and white pigeons flew away from his pipe. His grandfather saw the pigeons fly out of the lodge door, and he felt very sad. For he knew that his little grandson was a young man now, and would soon be leaving him. Then he went in, and they talked together for a long time. He told the young man all about the six giants who had killed his brothers and sisters, and White Feather said, "I shall go at once in search of them and kill them, because they were so cruel to all our tribe."

"No, do not go yet," said the old grandfather. "Wait awhile until you grow a little more and are stronger."

The young man promised to wait for a few months.

One day he was again hunting in the woods, when he passed near the wooden man. He heard him speak and say:

"White Feather, listen to me. In a few days you must go in search of the giants. They live in a high lodge in the centre of this wood. When you reach there, you must ask them to race with you, one at a time. Take this vine," handing him at the same time a thin, green vine. "It is enchanted, so they will not be able to see it. When you are running, throw it over their heads and they will trip and fall." White Feather thanked the old man, and took it home and showed it to his grandfather.

A few days later he set out in search of the giants. He had not journeyed far when he saw their lodge. When they saw him coming, they called out, "Oh, here comes White Feather. Here is the little man who is going to do such brave deeds." But when he came closer to them,they pretended they liked him, and told him how brave he was. They did that to make him think they were friends, but he did not believe them, as he knew they were his enemies. He asked them if they would race him, and they said, "Yes."

"Begin with the smallest of us," said the biggest giant. So they began. They had to run to a peel-tree and back again to the starting-point. This point was marked by an iron club, and whoever won the race was to take up the club and kill the other one with it. When they had nearly reached the peel-tree, White Feather threw the vine over the youngest giant's head. He tripped and fell. Then White Feather ran up and seized the club and killed the giant. The next day he raced the second youngest, and killed him in the same manner. Each day he did this, until only the biggest giant was left. Now this giant was the most dangerous of them all. He knew that, if he ran, White Feather would kill him, too, so he made up his mind that he would not race. White Feather said he was going home to see his grandfather before he ran this last race. As he was passing through the woods, the wooden man called to him.

"Listen to me," he said. "That tall giant is going to play a trick on you. When you are on your way back to his lodge, you will meet a most beautiful maiden. Do not listen to her, but change yourself into an elk. Remember this and obey me." The young man promised to remember. He spent the day with his grandfather, then made his way back to the giant's lodge. He had nearly reached it, when he saw the beautiful maiden coming towards him. She called to him, but he did not listen. He changed himself into an elk, and began eating the grass. Then she told him how mean he was to change himself into an elk, just because she was coming. He felt very sorry that she should think he was rude, and he wished he were a man again. At once he became himself, and began to talk to the maiden. Now she was really the big giant, who had changed himself into this form. After a while White Feather grew tired and lay down on the grass to sleep. When he was sound asleep, the maiden drew forth an axe and broke his back. She then changed him into a dog and herself back into the giant, who made the dog follow at his heels.

On the way to the giant's lodge, there was an Indian village where two sisters lived. They had heard of White Feather, and both wished that he would choose her for his wife. They looked out and saw the giant coming with the white feather in his hair, for he had taken the feather and put it in his own hair. They thought he was the brave warrior of whom they had heard so much. The elder sister had made her lodge look very gaudy, and had dressed herself in all her beads and quills. The younger sister had left her tent just as it was, and was dressed neatly. When the giant came along, he chose the elder sister. She would have nothing to do with the dog, but the younger sister felt sorry for it and let it come and live in her lodge.

The giant used to go hunting each day, but he never succeeded in killing very many animals. The dog used to go out also, and he always brought back a beaver, a bear, or some other animal for food. This made the giant and his wife jealous. So they made up their minds that they would tell the chief that his young daughter was treating a dog with too much kindness. When they had gone, the dog made signs to the maiden for her to sweat him the way the Indians do. She made a lodge for him just big enough to hold him. Then she heated some stones until they were very hot. She put these stones in the lodge beside him, and poured water on them. In a minute the lodge was full of steam. She closed the door and left him there. After a while he came forth, a handsome, young man, but he could not speak.

When the giant and his wife told the chief about the dog who was such a great wonder, he felt sure there was some magic in it. So he gathered a band of young men, and sent them to bring the daughter and the dog to his lodge. What was their surprise to find a handsome, young man instead of the dog. They all went together to the lodge of the chief, who had gathered together all the other men of the village, the giant among them. When the young man entered, he made a sign to put the white feather in his hair. The chief took it from the giant's head, and put it on the young man's. At once he was able to talk. He then told them to smoke from his pipe. It went around the circle until it reached him. When he began to smoke, blue and white pigeons flew from the pipe. Then everybody knew that he was the great warrior, White Feather.

The chief asked him to tell them all about himself. He did so very truthfully, and when the chief learned how wicked and cruel the giant had been, he ordered that he should be changed into a dog and let loose in the village, where the boys were to stone him to death. This order was carried out. A few days afterwards, White Feather said good-bye to the good old chief, and he and the kind maiden returned to his grandfather.

They found him waiting for them in the forest near the wooden man. The grandfather wept for joy when he heard that the last giant was dead. And the wooden man said, "Now my work is ended;" and with that he changed into a gnarled oak-tree with withered branches, which seemed to talk as the wind whistled through them.

The Lone Lightning

THERE once lived a lonely little boy whose father and mother were dead. His uncle took care of him, but did not treat him kindly. He made him work very hard and gave him little to eat. The little fellow grew very thin, and began to pine away.

Then his uncle changed his way of treating him and began to fatten him. He pretended that he was doing this to make the boy grow strong. But he really intended to kill him after a while. He told his wife to give the boy lots of bear meat to eat. He made him eat a lot of the fat as well. This is supposed to be the best part of the bear's meat.

One day the boy did not want to eat the fat. His uncle pushed some down his throat and nearly choked him. He managed to get away from his uncle, and ran out of the lodge. He ran as fast as he could, and by night he was many miles away. He found himself in a bush and was afraid to lie down on the grass for fear the wild beasts would come and eat him, so he climbed to the top of a tall pine-tree, and rested in its branches.

As he was sleeping he had a dream. He thought a spirit came from the upper world and said, "My dear child, I have seen how cruel your uncle has been to you, and how brave you are, so I have a deed I want you to do; come with me." Then the boy wakened and followed the spirit. They went high up in the sky and then the spirit said:

"Over in the north there live many Manitous. They are bad spirits and unfriendly to all that are good. Here are twelve magic arrows; shoot them at these spirits, and see if you can kill them."

He gave the arrows to the boy, and he at once began to shoot.

His first arrow did not hit any one, and as it flew through the air a long, single streak of lightning showed where it had gone. The next arrow was the same, so he kept on till eleven arrows had been shot. By this time the bad spirits were very angry. The chief of them called out, "I shall punish you for daring to aim your arrows at us." Just then the boy aimed the last arrow at the chief. As it came near, the spirit changed himself into a rock, and the arrow sank deep into its stony side. But at this instant the boy was changed into the lone lightning which may be seen in the northern sky on autumn nights.

The Enchanted Moccasins

ONCE on Mackinac Island there lived a little Indian boy and his sister. They saw only the birds and animals, for no human beings were there but themselves. The little boy, instead of playing with his sister, used to go into the forest and think. So she thought that he would grow up to be a very wise man and do some wonderful deeds. She called him Onwe Bahmondoong, which means, the boy that carries a ball on his back.

As he grew up, he was very anxious to know where the people lived. His sister told him that many miles away there was a village, where hundreds of warriors and hunters lived. He asked her to make him six pairs of moccasins, so that he could go and find the village. He then put some food in a bag, took his war-club, and, when the moccasins were finished, set out on his journey. As he was saying good-bye to his sister, she told him that one pair of the moccasins was enchanted.

On he went quickly, over miles of prairie, across little streams, and through the bush. When he grew tired, he would lie down and sleep. When he was rested, he would get up and go on. So he travelled many days, and when one pair of moccasins wore out, he put on another pair.

At last he came to a wigwam, in which sat an old woman. When she saw him, she called, "Come in, my grandchild."

He entered, and sat down at her feet.

"Where are you going?" she asked him.

"I am going to find the village of the hunters," he answered.

"Oh, beware, my child," she cried. "Many a brave one of your tribe has tried to find that village, and none has ever come back. Take care they do not kill you, also."

"I am not afraid," the boy replied, his eyes shining.

"Well, listen to me," she said in a low voice. "I shall give you two bones which the medicine men use. They will help you very much." Then she told him many things which he was to do when the time came. When she had finished, he thanked her, and went his way.

He travelled for two days more, and at last came in sight of the hunters' village. It looked as the old woman told him it would. In the centre of the village stood a lodge, where the chief lived. In front of this lodge, a tall tree grew. This tree was stripped of its bark and branches, and hanging from it, about halfway up, was a small lodge, wherein lived the chief's two daughters. It was in this small lodge that all the Indians had been killed, after they had found the village.

The boy remembered what the old woman had told him, so he changed himself into a squirrel. He ran up the smooth side of the tree. But when he had nearly reached the lodge, the tree shot quickly up into the air, carrying the little house with it. The boy climbed up higher. Again the tree shot up in the air. And the higher he climbed, the higher the tree went, until at last it stopped. It could go no farther, for it had reached the arch of heaven.

When the boy saw this, he changed himself from the squirrel back into a boy, and entered the lodge. The two sisters were squatted on the floor. He asked them their names. The one on the left said hers was Azhabee, which means, one who sits behind. The girl on the right said hers was Negahnahbee, which means, one who sits before. When he spoke to the girl on the left, the tree began to sink down. Then when he spoke to the other sister, it began to shoot up into the air again. When he noticed this, he continued talking to the girl on the left, and the tree kept on sinking lower, until at last it was down as it had been at first. Then the boy drew out his war-club.

"I am going to kill you," he said to the sisters, "for you have been so cruel to all my relatives." Swinging his club, he brought it down on their heads and killed them both. Then he jumped from the lodge to the ground.

As he stood there, he remembered that these two sisters had a brother and a father, who would be sure to kill him, when they found what he had done. So he turned, and ran very quickly. He had not gone far, when the father and brother returned. When they saw the dead girls, they were very angry. The father told the brother to follow the boy.

"It must be that boy who killed them," he said, "for he is the only stranger here. Follow him, and do not eat until you have killed him. If you eat, your power is gone."

The brother started off, running even faster than the boy. When the boy heard him coming, and knew that he would be caught, he climbed a tree. Then he began to shoot magic arrows back at the brother. But this did not seem to hurt him. So the boy got down from the tree, and ran on again. Now he could tell that the brother was very close to him. So he changed himself into a dead moose, and lay down on the grass. He drew out the enchanted moccasins, and whispered to them, "Travel on and on till you come to the end of the earth." Away they went, because they were enchanted, leaving their marks behind them.

When the brother came up he saw only a dead moose, with footmarks leading away from him. He followed on, until he came to the end of the earth. Then he saw that he had been fooled, that he had been following only a pair of moccasins. He was so very angry that he did not know what to do .And he felt tired and hungry. He thought surely he must eat now. Then he remembered his dead sisters, and said, "No, I shall find that boy yet, and kill him." So he turned back till he came to the spot where the dead moose had been. To his surprise it was gone, and footsteps led away in the opposite direction.

He followed them until he came to a beautiful, old garden, with fruit trees and flowers in it. In the garden stood an old house covered with vines, where a very old man lived. He was so very old that his two daughters did everything for him. Now this old man was really the boy, who had changed himself this way. The daughters saw the brother coming.

"Father," they said, "there is such a tired-looking traveller coming up the road. May we ask him in?"

"Yes, invite him to enter," answered the father, "and give him something to eat."

The daughters called to the brother, and invited him in. He was glad to enter the cool, shady garden. They cooked him some hot food and other nice things, and when he smelt the meal, he could not refuse to eat, for he had been without food for such a long time, and had travelled so many miles. He ate of the food, and as he did so, he forgot all about his dead sisters, forgot even his home. A strange, sleepy feeling came over him, and he fell into a sound sleep.

When the old man saw this, he changed himself back into a boy, and the garden, house, and daughters disappeared. Only the sleeping brother lay there. The boy quickly drew the ball around from his back, which turned out to be a magic war-club. With this he put an end to the brother. As he journeyed homewards through the forest he heard the sound of footsteps behind him. Turning, he saw nothing; but the sound was coming nearer. In a moment a pair of moccasins appeared on the path. It was the enchanted moccasins returning from the ends of the earth. The boy quickly picked them up and put them in his bag. Then he continued gladly on his way and soon reached the lodge, where his sister came forth to meet him. She was very proud of his brave deed, and she and the boy always treasured the enchanted moccasins.

The Five Water-spirits

ONCE upon a time a grey, old man lived on the top of a mountain, where he could see glimpses of the sea. He had a lodge made of birch bark that shone like silver in the sun.

He had five beautiful daughters, whose names were Su, Mi, Hu, Sa, and Er.[1]

One day the youngest said, "My sisters, come and we will go and play near the broad, blue sea, where the waves beat against the rocks." So away they ran out of the lodge and down the mountain side. They were all dressed in robes of snow-white foam, that fluttered far behind them as they ran. Their sandals were of frozen water-drops, and their wings of painted wind. On they scampered over valley and plain, until they came to a tall, bare rock as high as a mountain.

---

[1]Su, Superior; Mi, Michigan; Hu, Huron; Sa, St. Clair; Er, Erie.

Then the youngest cried, "Sisters, here is a dreadful leap, but if we are afraid, and go back, our father will laugh at us." So, like birds, they all plunged with a merry skip down the side of the rock. Then "Ha-ha," they cried, "let us try again." So up to the top they climbed, laughing with joy, and down once more they went, nor ever stopped, laughing like girls on a holiday.

The day wore on till sunset, and still they laughed and played. The round moon came up, and by its silvery light they sprang from the tall, bare rock, and climbed joyously up its side again.

Next morning, when the sun arose, the rock was no longer bare. Over its stony side poured great sheets of foaming water, and in the foam still played the five sisters. They never reached the sea, and there they still play, giving to us the beautiful Niagara Falls. Sometimes, if you look closely, their forms may be seen in the white foam, but always in the sunny spray you may see their sandals and their wings.

The Canoe Breaker

ONCE in a certain tribe there was a young man who had no name. For it was the law in that tribe that every youth had to do some deed that would give to him his name. This young man had tried in many ways to do something that would make the chief tell him that he was a great warrior. Several times he had tried to kill a bear, but had failed. He had gone forth in battle, hoping to kill some powerful enemy, but no one had fallen under his tomahawk. He had gone on long hunting trips, hoping to bring home the skin of some wild animal, but had always returned empty-handed. So his brave, young heart felt very sad, for the young men of the tribe laughed at him for not having won a name for himself.

One summer day, the tribe left their camp on the lake shore and went back among the hills on a hunting trip. After they had gone some distance, the young man left the others and wandered off by himself, hoping that this time he would kill some animal, and so be no longer scorned by his companions. He tramped for many hours through the forest and over the hills, without catching sight of anything. At length, he climbed one hill which was higher than the others, and from here he could see the small creek which flowed through the hills down to the lake. As he was looking at it, he thought he saw some dark objects along the shore of the creek. They seemed about the size of canoes. He scanned the hills anxiously, and at length could see a band of Indians making their way along the trail made by the hunters in the morning.

At once the young man knew there was great danger ahead, for these Indians, the Shuswaps, were the enemies of his tribe and now were following their trail, and when they found them, they would kill them. Quickly the young man made his way down the hill, and through the forest to the spot where the hunters had camped for their evening meal. Running up to them, he cried, "Return at once to your lodges. Our enemies are now on our trail. They are in the forest on the other side of this hill. I shall return and delay them while you reach your lodges in safety."

Then, without waiting for a reply, he turned and ran back in the direction from which he had come. By short cuts through the hills, he made his way to the creek and found, as he expected, that the Indians had left their canoes tied at its mouth. Seizing his tomahawk, he began to break the canoes, and soon had a hole made in all of them except one. Leaving the creek, he mounted the hill and from there could see the Shuswaps. He began to wave his arms and call wildly to attract their chief. At last they noticed him and began to make their way towards him. The young man was delighted, for now he knew that his tribe could escape in safety, while their enemies were returning towards the creek.

Soon the Shuswaps neared the top of the hill, and he knew he must think of some plan to delay them here. Suddenly he dropped to the ground and lay there as though insensible. With a run the Shuswaps gained the summit and surrounded him. He lay face downwards with his arms stretched out. They turned him over on his back and peered into his face. Not a muscle moved; not even his eyelids quivered. Then the chief bent over him and felt his heart. "He has not gone to the Happy Hunting Ground," he said, "but the Great Spirit has called his spirit to go on a long journey. It may not be back for many moons. Let us place his body under the pine-trees, there to await the return of the spirit."

The Indians lifted the body of the young man, carried it to a clump of pine-trees and laid it down. Then they walked some yards away and held a council.

As soon as they were a safe distance away, the young man jumped up. He ran down the hill, and reaching the canoes, jumped into the unbroken one and began to paddle down the creek.

The Shuswaps turned and saw him. With fierce cries, they began to race down the hillside, and when they arrived at the spot where they had left their canoes, and saw what had happened, they filled the air with their angry yells. The young man was now out on the lake in the canoe, and they were unable to follow him, as all the other canoes were wrecked. They ran angrily along the lake shore, thinking he would land on their side, but instead, he made his way across the lake to the other side.

When the young man reached the shore, he again seized his tomahawk, and this time broke the canoe with which he had saved his life. The defeated Shuswaps, standing on the shore, saw him do this, and again they filled the air with their angry yells. There was nothing for them to do but to return to their camp, while the young man made his way along the lake shore to the village of his tribe. When he reached there, he found that he was no longer a man without a name. His brave deed had won for him the name of Kasamoldin, — the canoe breaker, — and ever afterwards in his tribe, and to others, he was known by this name.

The Old Stump

LONG ago there was an old woman called Grizzly Bear. She had neither husband nor children, and lived all alone in a lodge on the hillside.

As the days went by, she became very lonely, and so she made up her mind to find a daughter for herself. She took some pitch and fashioned a girl out of it. Then she put this figure out beside the river, and it began to move and speak.

"You are my daughter now," Grizzly Bear said to the girl, "and you shall live with me in my lodge. Every day you may bathe in the river, but, when you have finished, you must come at once into the shade of the lodge, instead of drying yourself in the sunshine."

The girl promised to do this and for three days she obeyed her mother's commands, but on the fourth day she thought she would see what would happen to her, if she sat on the bank in the sunshine. So, when she had finished bathing, she seated herself on a stone by the river. The sun was very hot, and in a few minutes the young girl had melted and disappeared.

When Grizzly Bear learned what had happened, she felt very sorrowful, but she was still determined to find another daughter for herself.

This time she took some clay and fashioned a girl from it. When the girl moved and spoke, she told her she might bathe in the river every day and might seat herself in the sunshine to dry, but she must not rub herself while in the water. This command the girl obeyed for three days. On the fourth day, she thought she would see what would happen to her if she rubbed herself while she was in the water. So, when she went in to bathe, she began to rub herself and at once broke into pieces and melted away.

When Grizzly Bear saw what had happened, she again was very sorrowful, and this time she made up her mind to make a daughter who could not destroy herself. So, taking a block of wood, she fashioned a girl from it. When the wood came to life, Grizzly Bear told her that she might bathe every day in the river and bask in the sun if she liked.

The daughter did this for three days, and on the fourth, as she was standing by the riverside, she saw a large trout leap out the water.

"What a beautiful trout," said the girl to herself. "How I wish I had it."

Three times the trout leaped out of the water, and the fourth time it landed on the shore by her feet. At once it changed into a handsome, young man.

"Come with me," he said to the girl. "I have a beautiful home beneath the water. Come with me and be my wife, and you shall live happy all the rest of your days."

The girl said she would go. Then he told her to get on his back and to shut her eyes as he leaped into the water. She must keep them shut until he told her to look. She promised to obey him, but, scarcely were they beneath the water, when she opened her eyes to see where they were. At once she found herself alone on the bank of the river.

The next day the same thing happened. She opened her eyes before they had reached the underwater world, and again she found herself alone on the bank. This happened once more on the third day, but on the fourth she succeeded in keeping her eyes closed until her husband told her to open them.

She found herself in a beautiful country, much like the one she had come from. There were homes and gardens and children here, and she knew she would be very happy.

As the years went by, two children were born, a boy and a girl. One day they came to their mother and told her that the other children had taunted them with having no grandmother.

"Yes, you have a grandmother," she replied. "She lives in a lodge near the river. You may go above the water to-day and visit her home, but you must make sure first that she is digging roots on the hillside, for she must not see you."

The children promised and went at once above the water. They saw the lodge, and an old woman digging roots. Very quietly, they made their way to the home of their grandmother. They found some food on the table and helped themselves. Then they went back to tell their mother all they had seen.

Three days they did this, but Grizzly Bear had missed the food each day, and knew that no one but grandchildren would enter her lodge this way and take her food. So, the fourth day, she commanded an old stump to look like an old woman digging roots, and to move as the children passed. Going back to her lodge, she prepared some powerful medicine, and then hid herself behind some deerskins.

In a little while the children entered and began to eat the food. The old woman quickly sprang out and threw the medicine over them. The boy was completely covered with it, while only a few drops fell on the girl. At once the boy changed into his proper form, and was a handsome young Indian, while the girl was changed into a little black dog.

Grizzly Bear told the boy that she was his grandmother, and that he must live with her now, but she did not tell him that the dog was his sister. She only said, "You must take great care of this little dog, and never beat or ill use it."

The boy promised, and every day he would go forth with his bow and arrows to shoot birds, while the little dog ran beside him. One day he was shooting red-headed woodpeckers. Three times he had killed a bird, and the little dog ran ahead and ate it before he could reach her. The boy became very angry at this, and, when she did it for the fourth time, he struck her a hard blow with his arrow.

At once the dog cried, "Why are you treating me thus, and I am your sister?" As soon as she had said this, she ran away. The boy followed, but before he could catch it, the dog had turned into a chickadee and had flown away. The sorrowing boy returned to his grandmother, and told her everything that had happened.

"Why did you not tell me that the dog was my sister?" he asked.

"If I had told you," she replied, "you would have been more sorrowful than you are now." Then she added, "Listen to me, my grandson; when you are shooting, if an arrow should lodge in a tree where it is too high for you to reach, do not climb to get it."

The boy promised to remember this command, and three times when an arrow pierced a tree above his reach, he gave it up as lost, but the fourth time he forgot the command. Seeing his arrow only a few inches above his head in the bark of the tree, he began to climb for it. Just as his hand touched it, the arrow moved farther up. He climbed higher and, as he reached it, again it moved up. This went on until the arrow and the boy were out of sight in the clouds.

Neither the boy nor his sister was ever seen again, and Grizzly Bear, who had been watching from the ground, was left there all alone. And there she still stands, looking just like the stump of an old tree, but the Indians know who it is, and as they pass by, they place an offering on the withered stump.

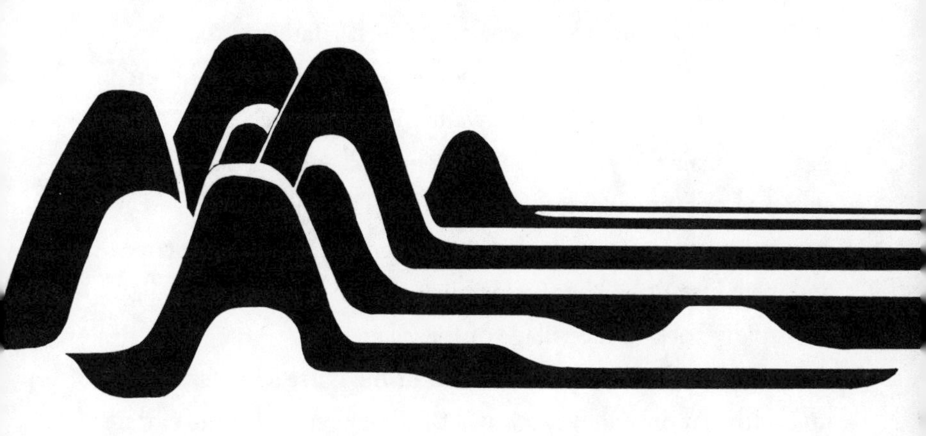

The Cliff of Sinikielt

ONCE long ago there was a chief of the Okanagan Indians called Tserman. He was very brave and very daring, and he stopped at nothing when he wanted to have his own way. The village of the Okanagans lay in a beautiful valley; to the north-west lay the hunting grounds of the Nicolas, who had been enemies of the Okanagans for years. Now the chief of the Nicolas had a lovely daughter, Lalita, and Chief Tserman fell in love with this beautiful maiden. He knew there was no use asking her father to give him Lalita, so he made up his mind to steal her.

One dark night he saddled his black pony, which could run faster than any other horse of the tribe, and, under cover of the darkness, he made his way over the hills and down the valley until he came to the camp of the Nicolas. All was very still in the camp, for it was late and the Indians were all tired, for they had just returned from a long hunting trip. Tserman could see the small, white lodge of Lalita close beside that of her father.

Leaving his horse standing beside a tall pine-tree, he crept cautiously towards Lalita's wigwam. When he reached the opening, he remained very still and listened. There was not a stir or sound of any one moving in the camp. Throwing aside the curtain, he quickly entered the lodge, snatched Lalita from her couch, and in an instant had her beside him on his horse and was galloping rapidly back to the village of the Okanagans.

The Nicolas, roused by the sound of the horse's hoofs, jumped up hastily. At once they knew what had happened, for the curtain of Lalita's lodge was still thrown back. The chief ordered his warriors to mount their ponies and quickly follow in pursuit. And soon, in the darkness, the sound of their ponies could be heard as they raced wildly after the flying chief. But Tserman's horse could run much faster than any horse in the mountains, and before the Nicolas were halfway to the village, he and Lalita were safe within his lodge. On came the Nicolas, and at last only one hill lay between them and the village of their enemies. To go around this hill would be many miles, so, leaving their horses at the foot, they began to climb its slippery side. At length they reached the top, but they did not know that this was a sheer cliff they had climbed, and that at its foot, between them and the Okanagan village, there flowed a deep river.

One of their warriors, Sinikielt, wanted to go ahead and find out the best way to reach the village and surround it. He crept forward in the darkness, and with a wild cry fell over the steep cliff into the river beneath. His cry rang out through the night and was heard by the Okanagans on the other side of the river. Quickly the camp was aroused, and going forth, the warriors encircled the hill. When the morning came, the Okanagans began to climb the hill to attack their enemies. The Nicolas saw them coming and knew there was nothing for them but certain death. The Okanagans were many and strong and were well armed. The Nicolas were only a few warriors, and if they remained to fight, they were sure of being either killed or taken prisoners. There was only one thing for them to do. Turning their backs on the fast-approaching enemies, they made one running leap from the cliff to the river below and sank forever in its waters.

Many years after, when Tserman had gone to the happy hunting ground and his son Lemichin was made chief in his stead, there came sad days to Lalita. Lemichin was a great warrior and strong and handsome like his father, but he cared nothing for the good of his tribe. His only thought was his own pleasure. Little by little he gambled away all his possessions, until nothing was left but his saddle-horse. Then one night that was lost too. Lalita begged him to turn from his evil ways, but he made her no reply. Going forth from the lodge, he made his way to the hills and remained there for one moon. At the end of that time he returned to the tribe. Going to his mother, he said:

"Lalita, when I was in the hills, I fasted and then I slept, and in my dreams my father came to me. He told me what to do to make my evil life turn into a good one. First, I must make peace with the Nicolas. After that I must win my way back until I am a great chief, like my father was before me."

"My son," said Lalita, "this is indeed a happy thing you have told me, and great indeed is the spirit of your father which has come to you and told you what to do."

The next day Lemichin sent a messenger of peace to the Nicolas. Their old chief, Lalita's father, sent back word that there would be no more fighting between the tribes, but that the Nicolas and the Okanagans could never be friends. Lemichin made no answer when this message was brought to him. Going forth, he began gambling again. Lalita followed him and begged him to return with her, to forsake these evil ways. But to her also he made no reply. Day after day he gambled, but now he was not losing his possessions, but was winning them back again. At last they were all won, and then Lemichin called a council of his wisest warriors. He told them he wished to win the friendship of the Nicolas, and that he and Lalita would go to their village and take with them a large number of the herd as a gift. The next morning they set out, — Lemichin and Lalita riding ahead and three herd-boys, driving the greater part of the herd, followed behind. When they reached the village of the Nicolas, Lemichin told his mother to wait with the herd-boys, and dismounting from his pony, he went alone and on foot to the lodge of the old chief. Kneeling before the old warrior, he gave himself up to make reparation for the deed of his father Tserman.

The old chief was very angry at first and called his warriors to bind Lemichin and kill him. But Lemichin asked him to let him speak first. Then he told him how sorry his father had been for what he had done. How much he wished that the two tribes might become friends, and how anxious Lalita was to win the love of her father again. Then he asked him to accept the herd which he had brought with him. The old chief felt his anger fade away when the young man talked, and now, when he saw what a great gift he had brought with him, he felt that he could not kill so generous and manly a warrior. So, taking Lemichin by the hand, he walked with him to where Lalita sat on her pony.

When she saw her father Lalita uttered a cry of joy. The old man fondly embraced his daughter and said:

"My daughter, many moons ago you left your father's lodge and joined the tribe of our enemies. But this day your son has proven to me that our enemies can be brave and generous. My heart has been lonely all the summers and winters since you went away. Come now, you and your brave son, and live with the old chief so that his heart and his lodge shall no longer be empty." And weeping for joy, the old man led Lalita and Lemichin to his lodge. Thus friendship between the Nicolas and the Okanagans was established.

That was many years ago, but yet in the night the wild cry of Sinikielt answers the cry of the loon, and is echoed from the cliff far out across the river.

The Strange Dream

A WARRIOR and his wife once had a beautiful boy, for whom they made many plans. But when he grew up, and reached the right age, he would not consent to the fast. They wished him to blacken his face with charcoal, and not to eat anything for three days. But he threw away the charcoal, and when they denied him food, he ate birds' eggs and the heads of fish which had been cast away.

At length one day he came home, and, taking some coals, blackened his face. Then he went out of the lodge and lay down on the grass to sleep. As he lay there, he had a wonderful dream. He thought a beautiful maiden came to him, and said, "Onawa-taquto, come with me. Step in my tracks." He arose and did so, and felt himself mounting up over the tree-tops, until he reached the sky.

The maiden entered through a small opening, and he followed her. Looking around, he found himself on a beautiful, grassy plain. A tall lodge stood in the distance. She led him to it, and he saw that it was divided into two parts. In one end there were bows, arrows, clubs, and spears, and other things that belong to a warrior. In the other end were strings of colored beads, bright pieces of cloth, and fancy moccasins, such as belong to a maiden. On a frame was a broad belt, beautifully colored, that she was weaving.

"My brother will soon be home," she said, "and I do not wish him to see you, so come until I hide you." She put him in a corner and spread the belt over him.

In a short time the brother returned, and sat down in his end of the lodge. He took down his pipe, and began to smoke. Then, in a little while, he said, "Sister, when are you going to stop this practice? Do you forget that the Greatest of the Spirits has forbidden you to take the children of the earth? I know whom you have behind that belt. Come forth, Onawataquto."

When the young man came forth, he presented him with bows and arrows and a pipe of red stone. Now this meant that he was married to the maiden.

After that the brother used to take him with him over the beautiful plains, and he found everything very peaceful. Then he began to notice that the brother left the lodge each morning, and did not return until night. He asked him what he did when he was away.

"Come with me, and I shall show you," said the brother.

So they set off early next morning, and walked on for a long time. At last Onawataquto began to feel hungry.

"Wait a few minutes," said the brother, "and I shall show you how I get food."

When they reached a spot where they could see down to the earth below, he said, "Now sit down and watch." And Onawataquto did so.

When he looked down, he could see the earth quite plainly. In one village he saw a war party getting ready. In another he saw them dancing, and in another, a group of children playing beside a lodge.

"Do you see that beautiful boy down there?" asked the brother.

"Yes," he replied. Suddenly the brother darted something from his hand at the child, and he fell senseless.

The parents rushed out and carried him into the lodge, and made great wailing. Then they saw people gather around the lodge, and the medicine man arrived. He addressed himself to the spirit brother, and asked him what sacrifice he desired.

"I shall allow the boy to get better if you will make me the sacrifice of a white dog," answered the brother, through the opening in the sky.

They at once caught a white dog, and killed and roasted it. The meat was then put on dishes, which at once floated up to the spirit brother.

"Now eat," he said to Onawataquto. "This is the way I get all my meals."

After a while the young man grew tired of the quiet days, and desired to back to the earth. His wife was angry when she heard him say this, and said she would not let him go. But after a while she consented, and said, "You may go; but remember you are not to marry any of the earth maidens, for at any time I can draw you back here."

Next morning Onawataquto found himself lying on the grass by his father's lodge, with his face still blackened. His father and mother and all his friends were standing near him in glad surprise. They told him he had been away a year.

For some days he went around very quietly; then he began to forget his dream. After a while he could hardly remember it at all.

In a few months, he married one of the maidens of the tribe. That night he went out of his father's lodge, and was never seen again.

It is said that the spirit maiden had drawn him back to her home in the sky.

Big Chief's Conquest

ONCE in the long ago there lived a great warrior named Milkanops. He lived in a land of high, rocky mountains, and to the far north there lived a tribe of fierce, warlike Indians who were the enemies of his tribe. Many battles were fought between the two tribes, but Milkanops always won. At last, one autumn day, they fought from sunrise to sunset, and although Milkanops won the victory once more, he received his death wound. The poisoned arrow pierced his side just as the battle was won.

His warriors carried him to his lodge and laid him on his couch of deerskins.

"Send for my son," he told them. "Send for Aseelkwa." At once they brought the young warrior to his father's side.

"My boy," said the dying chief, "I have been called to the

happy hunting ground, and soon my spirit will be wandering with the happy ones there. Before I go, I wish to ask one thing of you. Promise me that you will not be a warrior as I have been, but will live to be a great chief, for that is what your name means, — Aseelkwa, Big Chief. Yonder to the north are enemies, and they will want you to go to war with them, as I have done many times. Do not listen to their challenges, but try to keep peace between the tribes and make your tribe great and good, rather than strong and warlike."

The young boy, weeping, promised his father to obey his commands, and not long after, the spirit of Milkanops started on its journey to the happy hunting ground.

As the months went by the enemies of Aseelkwa made many attempts to engage in war with him and his tribe, but to all of these challenges he gave no reply. A few years went by, and now the young boy was a full-grown warrior, but he did not call himself one. To all who spoke of him as a warrior, he would make answer that he was a chief and would not engage in battle. His enemies could not entice him, so they said he was a coward, and taunted him and said he was afraid to fight them.

One day one of the wise men came to Aseelkwa and said, "Oh, Big Chief, Hahola, the Rattlesnake, is a traitor. He has told our enemies that you are indeed a coward, as they say you are, and they have planned to attack our camp when the moon has faded to a narrow band in the sky."

"And Hahola, is he going to help them?" asked the chief, in a stern voice.

"Yes, O Great Chief. He will let them know when you are fast asleep in your lodge. Then, in the darkness, they will surround it and take you prisoner."

"It is well you have told me," said the chief. "Now I must fast and dream and see what I am to do."

So for nine days he fasted and dreamed. Then, after that time, he called his medicine men and said, "I have fasted and dreamed, and in my dreams I saw the spirit of my father Milkanops. He told me that I must not fight these enemies, but that I and my tribe must journey to the far south and there find a new hunting ground."

Early the next morning Aseelkwa and the tribe set out on their journey. For many days and many nights they travelled. They crossed rivers and climbed steep hills, and at length they reached a land where the hills were lower and greener than their rocky mountains had been. In front of them lay a very long, narrow valley with low hills on either side, and, just behind these, there rose one larger than the others, a tall, rocky mountain.

"In my dreams," said Aseelkwa, "I saw this long, narrow valley and that tall hill, and the spirit of my father told me that here we must make our new camp and hunt in these green hills."

The Indians were glad to know they had reached the end of their journey, for they were footsore and weary. Quickly they built their lodges on the hillside and went forth in search of food.

That night Aseelkwa called his medicine men to go with him to the top of the high hill, and there hold a council. He knew that Hahola, the Rattlesnake, would have told of their departure, and by this time the northern Indians would be well on their way in pursuit. Aseelkwa seated himself at the foot of a tall pine-tree, and the medicine men placed themselves in a circle around him. The night was dark, for the moon was only a narrow band in the sky. They had made no fire, for fear their enemies might see it. Scarcely had Aseelkwa begun to speak when a slight noise was heard. It sounded like some loosened stones falling down the mountain side. At once every warrior was on his feet and peering through the darkness.

"Look," said Aseelkwa. "There at the foot of the hill creeps away Hahola, the Rattlesnake. Our enemies are in hiding. Let us go down to them."

Down the hill they came, but before they reached the bottom, from behind every pine-tree and every stone there leaped a warrior, with fiendish yells. Out rang the war-whoop of Aseelkwa, and from every lodge there sprang forth the warriors who had fought for Milkanops, his father. Then, in the darkness, there followed a terrible battle. Many warriors fell on both sides, struck down with tomahawks. For some time it seemed as if the enemy must win. Then, little by little, Aseelkwa's army began to drive them back. At last they had them at the entrance to the narrow valley, and there was fought the fiercest part of the battle. But at last the enemy were forced out of the valley, and once in the open, they turned and vanished in the darkness. During this last fight Aseelkwa had been missing, and now his warriors began to search for him among the wounded. At last they found him, and there at his side lay Hahola, dead.

"Lift me up," said Aseelkwa, "and carry me to the high hill, and there lay me under the pine-tree." They did as he commanded, and after they laid him down he turned to them and spoke in a very weak voice.

"My warriors," he said, "in a few moments my spirit shall have gone to join that of my fathers in the happy hunting grounds. I dreamed of this battle, and everything has been just as I dreamed. Our enemies are defeated, and Hahola, the traitor, is dead. Bury him where he fell in the valley. By morning you will find that the Great Spirit has placed a barrier between you and your enemies, over which they can never cross. And remember, my brave warriors, that although I am not with you, that always shall the spirit of Aseelkwa watch over his tribe. You shall fight no more battles, but instead shall cultivate and make fruitful these hills."

Then he sank back upon the grass, and his spirit passed to the happy hunting grounds.

The warriors buried him where he lay, and then, as he had commanded them, buried Hahola in the narrow valley. When the sun rose next morning, they knew what Aseelkwa had meant, for where the valley had been the night before, there now was a long, narrow lake, whose still, blue waters told nothing of its great depth, for in the centre of this lake, just where Hahola was buried, there is no bottom to be found. Then the warriors looked up on the high hill and again they knew what Aseelkwa had meant. For, from the topmost point of the high rock, Aseelkwa's face, carved in stone, looked down over the lake and valley. There, calm and serene and peaceful, it still watches over the hills that have been made fruitful, over the tribe that is always at peace, and over the lake whose deep, blue waters are always ready to frown on the canoes of their enemies.

The Red Swan

THREE brothers, who were hunters, once lived together in a forest. They were very skilful and always returned well laden from the chase. One day they all agreed to go hunting. They were each to kill the animals that they usually killed, and then see who could get back to the lodge first and have the game cooked. So they took their finest arrows, and off they went.

The youngest brother, whose name was Odjibaa, had not gone far when he saw a bear. Now this was one animal that he was not supposed to kill, but he forgot his bargain and shot it. Then everything seemed to grow red, and he heard a queer noise. He followed it, and as he tramped on, the noise seemed closer. At last he came to the edge of the lake and there, floating on the water, was a beautiful Red Swan. Every once in a while it uttered the queer noise he had been hearing. He shot an arrow at the bird, but it flew past her. He shot another and another. They all fell near her, but she was quite unharmed. She swam around in the water, bending her head and arching her neck and not even noticing Odjibaa. This made him want her more than ever, so he shot the rest of his arrows. Still she was untouched.

Then he remembered that, in his dead father's medicine sack, there were three magic arrows, so he ran back at once to the lodge and took them. When he again reached the shore of the lake, he put one in his bow. He took good aim and shot. It came close to the bird. The second arrow came closer, and the third went through her neck. She did not fall into the water, but rose slowly into the air, and flew away towards the setting sun, with the arrow still in her neck.

Odjibaa waded into the lake and picked up the two magic arrows which were floating on the water. When he reached the shore again, he set out to follow the Red Swan. He was a great runner, for when he shot an arrow ahead of him, he could run so fast that it fell behind him.

So now he ran at his greatest speed. But the Red Swan was already out of sight. On he went through the forest, across streams, and over the prairie. At nightfall he reached a town where many Indians lived. The chief made him welcome and let him stay the night. In the morning, he set out once more, and by night he had reached a second town. He stayed there till morning and then continued his race.

By the next night, he had reached a lodge where a magician lived. The old man treated him very kindly. He made him sit down by the fire. Then he spoke a few words, and a metal pot with legs walked out and stood by the fire. He spoke a few more words and put one grain of corn and one berry into the pot. At once it became full of porridge. He told Odjibaa to eat this, and when he had done so, the pot became full again. It continued to do this until Odjibaa had eaten all he could. Then the magician told the hunter to lie down and rest, and in the morning he said to him:

"My grandchild, you are in search of the Red Swan. Be brave and travel on, and at last you will be successful. When you near the end, you will come to a lodge of another magician, and he will tell you what to do."

Odjibaa thanked the old man, and went once more on his way.

When he had gone some distance, he shot an arrow ahead of him and it fell behind him, so he knew that he was still going his best. He went on for some days and at last saw the lodge of the magician. This second old man was as kind as the first and treated him in much the same way. He gave him food from a magic kettle exactly like the first, and then bade him stay the night. Then in the morning he said to him:

"My grandchild, you are following the Red Swan. Many a hunter has done the same and has never returned. For she is the sister of a great chief. He once had a wampum cap which was fastened to his scalp. One day some warriors came and told him that the daughter of their chief was very sick. She said the only thing that would cure her was this cap of wampum and that the sight of it would make her better at once. The chief did not like to lend his cap, for if he took it off, his head would be bare and bloody. But he thought again of the sick girl and at last gave it to the warriors.

"That is many years ago, but they have not returned the cap yet. They were cheats and are keeping it to make fun of it. They carry it from one village to another to dance around it, and at every mean thing they say, the old man groans with pain. Many young men have tried to get it for him, but all have failed. He has offered many gifts to the one who gets it, and even the Red Swan will belong to the successful one. She is a very beautiful maiden, and for her many young men have risked their lives. You are very brave and will face great dangers. Go as you have come, and you will be the one to win the precious wampum."

So Odjibaa travelled for several more days. At last he saw a lodge, but before he came up to it he could hear the groans of some one inside. Coming up to the door, he knocked, and a voice bade him come in. On entering he saw a very old man seated in one corner. His face was withered and his head bare and bloody. He seemed to be in great pain.

The young man spoke kindly to him and asked him how he lost his scalp. Then the old man told his story: how the young men had cheated him, and how they were abusing the scalp now. Odjibaa looked very sorry, and when the old man saw this, he began to coax him to try and get it back. He promised him blankets and many other things that make an Indian rich. But he did not mention the Red Swan. Odjibaa noticed that a wall divided the lodge into two parts. He guessed that the Red Swan was behind the wall, for he thought he heard her dress rustle. After he had talked with the old man, and had learned many things about the unfriendly Indians, he said:

"I shall go in search of the cap. When you hear the noise of a hawk, put your head out of the door, so I may put the scalp on you quickly."

Early next morning he set out, and before the day was over had come near the Indian village. As he drew near he could hear the sound of much shouting, and in a few minutes could see hundreds of warriors dancing and yelling around a pole. On the top of this pole was the scalp. He changed himself into a humming-bird and flew by their heads. When they heard the soft, humming noise, they said, "What is that?" He flew on, until he came near the pole. Then he changed himself into a blue butterfly and fluttered up to it. He took the scalp in his mouth and lifted it from the pole. A mighty shout went up from the Indians when they saw what was happening. But they could not reach the butterfly, as it was so high up in the air. It began to float slowly away with the scalp. This was hard work, and the load was almost too heavy for Odjibaa, but he hung on until he was safe outside the village. Then he changed himself into a hawk and flew rapidly away. When he came near the lodge of the old man, he uttered the cry of the hawk. The old man put his head out, and with a great blow Odjibaa clapped his scalp on. The old man fell senseless and lay very still for a long time.

Odjibaa entered the lodge and sat down to wait. At length the old man opened his eyes and arose. But he was no longer an old man. Instead there stood a handsome, young warrior. He reached out his hand to Odjibaa and said:

"I can never thank you for all you have done for me. See, you have given me back my youth and strength. Now I shall never grow old. You must stay and live with me and I shall make you a great chief." Odjibaa replied:

"No, I must go back to my brothers. I shall leave early to-morrow morning." Then the magician began to get ready a bundle for Odjibaa. He put blankets, beads, feathers, and paints in it, but he said no word about the Red Swan, and Odjibaa did not like to ask him. The next morning the hunter said good-bye to the magician and prepared to go.

"Wait, my friend," he said, as he opened the door in the wall. A beautiful maiden stepped forth. "This is my sister, Red Swan. She is to be yours, as you saved my scalp."

Odjibaa was overjoyed at this. He thanked the magician again then taking the maiden by the hand, they set out for his home.

The Whispering Grass

ONCE, many long years ago, there was a green hill covered with long grass, which whispered and talked as the wind blew through it. It was the great friend of all the animals, especially the wild deer, the grey wolf, and the fox.

One summer day the whispering grass was very excited. The south wind had brought strange news to it, and now, as the sun rose up to noonday, they could see this strange thing for themselves. It meant great danger to their friends the animals, and they must send a message to warn them. So the grass called to the butterflies, and told them to go at once to the deer, the wolf, and the fox, and tell them to come to the green hill. Away flew the butterflies, and soon the animals had gathered to hear what this message might mean.

"Listen, my brothers," said the whispering grass. "There is great danger for you this day, for across the prairie there comes a band of hunters to take your lives."

"Hunters? What are they?" asked the animals. "We have never heard of such things."

"They are Indians," returned the grass, "with bows and arrows — deadly arrows that will pierce your hearts. These hunters are very near, and once they see you they will shoot their arrows at you, and that is your end."

"What must we do?" asked the animals. "You are wise, whispering grass; tell us what we may do to save ourselves."

"Go to your homes," answered the grass, "and remain there until sundown to-morrow. If all is safe, I shall send my messengers, the butterflies, to you at that hour to tell you to come to me."

The animals did as they were commanded, and by the time the hunters reached the foot of the hill, there was nothing living to be seen but some dainty butterflies that hovered above the grass. The remainder of that day and all the next the hunters searched for game in the hills, but not a deer could they see, not a wolf, not a fox. In the late afternoon they returned to their camp at the foot of the hill. They were tired and very hungry, for they had not brought food with them, as they expected to find game.

"Let us return," said one hunter. "There is no game in this land, and I am hungry. Let us go back to our village."

"Not so," said the second hunter. "Let us wait until to-morrow. Perhaps to-morrow we shall see game."

"Yes, let us wait until to-morrow," said a third hunter, "and to-night we shall eat grass. See, yonder is a hill well covered with grass. If the animals eat it, why cannot we?"

"But it is whispering grass," said the first hunter, in a low voice. "And he who eats of whispering grass can no longer kill anything with his arrows."

"Not so, brother," said the second hunter. "It is not whispering grass. Listen; there is a west wind blowing through it, and yet we can hear no sound of whispering."

They all listened intently, and as the second hunter had said, there was no sound of whispering. The wind was waving the grass blades and bending them low, and not a sound came from them.

"You are right. It is not whispering grass," said the first hunter, "and I am hungry; let us eat."

So they all gathered many handfuls of the green grass, and putting it into a pot, they boiled it, then gathering around the pot, they ate the grass with much relish. Then, rolling themselves in their deerskins, they fell asleep.

It was now the sunset hour; so, calling the butterflies to it, the whispering grass gave them a message for the animals.

"Go to your brothers," it said ,"and tell them all is safe now; that at sunrise to-morrow morning they may come forth from their homes and wander as usual among the hills. Their enemies, the hunters, will try to shoot them with their arrows, but they must not be afraid, for now these arrows can never touch them."

The butterflies flew away quickly and gave the message to the deer, the wolf, and the fox.

At sunrise the next morning the animals came forth gladly, and they had not gone far, when they saw the hunters coming towards them. Remembering the message of their friend, the grass, they did not fear to remain, and soon saw that the grass had been right. The hunters aimed their arrows at them and shot, but every arrow flew through the air and fell harmlessly at their feet. All day this strange thing happened, and at last the hunters, tired and discouraged, went back to their camp at the foot of the hill.

"My brothers," said the first hunter, "that was indeed whispering grass which we ate last night. For see, all day our arrows have failed to hit their mark, though the game has been many."

"Why did the grass not whisper, then?" asked the second hunter. "It deceived us."

"Yes, it deceived us," said the third hunter. "It kept silence while we listened, so that we might be tempted to eat of it. Now we have lost our power of hunting and shall be laughed at by the other hunters."

"We must fight this whispering grass," said the first hunter. "Let us go and pull it up by the roots, so that never again it may be able to deceive any hunter."

"Let us wait until the moon rises high in the sky," said the second hunter. "Then, indeed, we shall uproot the whispering grass and leave the green hill bare and naked."

The butterflies, who had been hovering near, heard what the Indians were saying, and now they flew with all speed to the animals and told them what was going to happen to the whispering grass.

"Oh, my brothers," said the butterflies, "your enemies, the hunters, have planned to kill the whispering grass to-night. Can you not save it?"

"We must save it," said the deer. "The whispering grass is our friend. It saved our lives, and now we must save it." Turning to the fox, the deer said, "Oh, brother, you are wise and great. Can you not think of a plan to save the grass?"

"I am not wise enough for that," said the fox, "but I know one who is wise. You, my brothers, remain here, while I run with all speed to the Dark Hills where the Manitou of the Bright Fire lives. He is wise and great, and he will help us."

Saying this, the fox ran at full speed in the direction of a long line of hills, and it was not long before he reached a small opening which led down under them. Entering this, he found himself in a long passage, at the end of which a red light could be seen. When he reached the end of the passage, he found himself in a large, low cave. In the centre of this cave a bright red fire glowed, and by its light he could see a dark figure seated on the floor near the fire. It turned its face as the fox entered, and he saw the kind face of the Manitou of the Bright Fire.

"You have come to me for help," said the Manitou, in a deep, soft voice. "What is wrong, my brother?"

"Our friend, the whispering grass, is going to be uprooted to-night by the hunters," said the fox. "Can you tell us how to save the grass, for it has been kind and has saved us from these same hunters?"

"My brother," said the Manitou, "do you see these things which look like dark stones?" As he said this, he pointed to where a heap of black objects resembling stones was lying on the floor of the cave. "I have gathered these from the bowels of the earth. Many years ago Gitche Manitou, the Mighty Spirit, put them there. He took pieces of the midnight sky and mixed with each piece a million sunbeams. Then He hid these deep in the earth, where man would find them when he needed light and heat. I shall place some of these dark stones in my fire, while you return to your brothers, the wolf and the deer. Bid them return with you, and when you again reach my cave these stones shall be ready for you. Now go, and waste no time, for you must have everything ready before the hunters awaken."

The fox needed no second bidding. Away he went like the wind. When he reached the deer and the wolf, he found them anxiously waiting for him. Quickly giving them the Manitou's message, they all ran back to the cave. When they reached it, they found that the Manitou had placed a number of the dark stones in his fire, and that now they were no longer dark stones but bright red ones.

"My children," said the Manitou, "take these burning coals and place them in a circle on the hillside among the whispering grass. They will not harm the grass and their heat will not burn you as you journey back. But after this, always beware of a glowing fire, for I can give you my protection this time only."

The animals at once seized as many of the burning coals as they could carry and raced back to the hill. The night was dark, as the moon had not yet risen, and when at length they gained the hillside, they saw that the hunters still slept. Obeying the Manitou, they placed the coals in a circle on the side of the hill, and then hid behind some trees.

Scarcely had they done this, when the hunters awakened. At once they noticed the strange, glowing circle on the hillside. They rubbed their eyes and looked again; it was still there, burning and yet having no flame. Terrified, they gazed at it, not daring to climb the hillside. At last one said:

"My brothers, let us return at once to our village. This whispering grass must be a great friend of Gitche Manitou, and we have done wrong to eat of it. Let us return and warn our brothers."

"You are right, my brother," said the other hunter. "We will return and tell of this strange, terrible warning which Gitche Manitou has sent to us."

So saying, they turned and disappeared rapidly in the darkness, while the circle on the hillside glowed brightly until the sun rose. When daylight came there was nothing to be seen of the coals, but on the hillside where they had been there was a large, brown circle, which could be seen quite plainly from the valley. And there it can be seen to this day. On climbing the hill, the circle vanishes, and not a spot of burnt grass is to be found, but always from the valley below the brown circle can be seen. And the animals from that night have been afraid of glowing fire, for they know the Manitou cannot give his protection another time.

But he has been their greatest friend ever since that night. When they are in any trouble they go at once to the Dark Hills, and, creeping through the long passage, reach the cave where the bright fire glows. There they tell the kind Manitou all that makes them sad, and he comforts them. In the autumn he tells the deer where to hide in the hills, so that the hunters cannot kill them. In the long, cold winter he tells the hungry grey wolf where to find food, and in the summer he shows the red fox how to double on his trail so that none may catch him. And to all of them he has taught the secret of the glowing fire, that its brightness means danger, save when they rest beside it in his cave under the Dark Hills.

The Legend of Mackinac Island

MANY years ago, a party of wild Ojibwa Indians were resting on the shore of Lake Huron. The story-tellers of the tribe were telling many of their magic tales. One of them spoke, and said, "A wigwam stands in the deep. At the bottom of the lake a big turtle lies asleep in this wigwam. Around him swim white fish and trout, and the slow-worm goes creeping by. The scream of the sea gull and the shouts of the rovers do not waken him. Nothing can disturb his slumber but the magic song."

Then one of the Indians spoke, "Let us sing the magic song. Let us waken this big turtle from his long sleep."

So they all began to sing a strange, wild song. The sound floated out over the quiet waters of the lake. Suddenly the waves began to rise and roll to the shore, although there was no wind blowing. The centre of the lake seemed to rise higher; then slowly there appeared above the waters the curved back of the big turtle called Mishini-Makinak, toiling up to answer their call. Then the dragging tail appeared like a fleshy cape, and the jowl like a headland of dark rock. The Indians stood along the shore, staring in frightened surprise, as the monster arose like an island in the midst of the waves.

As the days went by, the turtle called his children from their silent homes to come and play around him. Up the lake and down over the falls came the dappled trout and the white fish, to play in the silvery tide, and by night the fairies danced on the rocky cliffs. For many days the red men watched eagerly, afraid to go to the magic island, but at last they paddled their birch-bark canoes across the waves to the pebbly beach. From that time Mishini-Makinak was their home.

The Adventures of Wesakchak

The Wonderful Ball

Wesakchak was once the only person living. He found himself floating all alone on the water. Above him was the sky, and all around and about stretched water. He called aloud, but no one answered. Then he noticed a little, dark object floating near him. It was a rat.

"My little brother," said Wesakchak, "we are all alone in this world of sky and water."

"Yes," said the rat. "But I am not afraid, for you are with me. Are you afraid?"

"No," said Wesakchak, "for the Mighty One will take care of us both. Do you go below and see if you can find any land."

The rat quickly obeyed Wesakchak and sank down through the water in search of dry land. He was gone a long time, and Wesakchak, began to wonder if he was ever coming back. At last he floated up, but was dead, and in his paws there was a little bit of clay. Wesakchak was very sorry when he saw that his little comrade was dead. He took the clay from the rat's paws and breathed upon it. Now Wesakchak was greater than a human being; he was really a spirit. So when he breathed upon the clay, it formed itself into a ball and began to grow. He rolled the ball in his hands, and when it grew a little larger, he said a few words over it. At once there came forth a little mouse, who began running around the ball. The mouse was just the color of the earth. Wesakchak said to it, "Your name shall be The Mouse and you shall always live amid the people, and your color shall be the color of the earth." So to this day we find the mouse in the homes of people, and it always is the same dark grey color.

As the mouse continued running, the ball kept growing. In a few minutes Wesakchak said some more words and out ran a little chipmunk. He began chasing around the ball too, but he could not stay on as well as the mouse. He slipped and nearly fell off several times. Wesakchak caught him and put him safely on again, but in doing so left the marks of his fingers on the chipmunk's back. And there they have remained ever since, and look like dark brown stripes.

The two little animals kept on running and Wesakchak now brought forth a red squirrel. There was a strong wind blowing, and the squirrel seemed timid. He would run for a little distance and then sit down. The wind would catch his bushy tail and blow it up over his head as he sat there, and so ever afterwards the squirrel curled his tail up when he sat down.

The ball kept growing larger and larger, and Wesakchak brought forth one animal after another. The rabbit, the fox, the wolf, the bear, and all the rest of them came out as they were called, until at last the ball was as big as the earth. Then he called forth the moose, and when it came and saw miles and miles of prairie, it ran for five miles without stopping. To this day the moose, when chased, always runs five miles before it stops.

When Wesakchak had all the animals on the earth, he gave them all their homes. Some were to live in the forests, some among the mountains, and others were to live on the prairies. He made little creeks to flow to divide their feeding-grounds, and they were told not to cross these water lines. The water in the creeks was not clean. It had green slime floating on the top, and reeds and rushes grew thickly amongst it. He made the water this way because he did not wish the animals to drink it. Then he made beautiful, clear rivers flow through the land to be their drinking water. In the rivers he made fish swim, and called all the animals who lived on fish to come and live near the banks of the rivers. In the trees he told the birds to build their nests, and soon all the animals and birds were happy and contented in their homes.

They all loved Wesakchak, for he was so wise and good. He was kind to them all and called them his brothers. He knew the secrets of the animals: why the moose is ungainly and has no flesh on his bones, why the rabbit's ears are long and have each a little roll of flesh behind it, and why the rat has no hair upon its tail. He understood all the languages of the animals, and each came to him when it was in trouble.

There was one animal who was very smart and clever. He was

about the size of the wolf and was called the wolverine. He had beautiful, soft fur, long, straight legs, and firm feet. But he was not liked by the other animals, for he was very conceited. He was always talking about his beautiful fur and his long legs. He would ask the other animals to race with him, because he knew he could always win. Then he would laugh at them for not being able to run as fast as he could. He was always getting into mischief, too, and never seemed happy unless he was playing a trick on some other animal. The other animals often came and told Wesakchak how mean the wolverine was to them. He would tell them to try to be patient, and then he would scold the wolverine for being so unkind. The wolverine would pretend he was very sorry, but the very next day he would do some more mean tricks.

One day he came past the wigwam of Wesakchak. Looking in, he saw that it was empty, and that the Fire Bag, where Wesakchak always kept his steel and flint and his pipe and tobacco-pouch, was hanging on the wall. The wolverine looked around and saw that no one was near, so he sneaked in and grabbed the bag. He ran away through the bush with it until he came to a tall tamarac tree. He climbed the tree and hung the bag on one of the branches. Then he jumped down and ran away, laughing to himself at the trick he had played on Wesakchak.

When Wesakchak returned home, it was nearly evening, and he was tired and hungry. He looked around for his Fire Bag, for he wished to make a fire. The way they got a spark in those days was to strike the steel and flint together; a spark would fly forth and set the dry bark on fire. But Wesakchak could not find his bag. He looked all over the wigwam, still he could not find it. Then he noticed footmarks on the ground near the door. Looking closely, he saw whose they were. "It is that mischief-maker, the wolverine, who has taken my bag," he said. "I shall go in search of it. And if I meet him, I shall punish him well for all his mischief-making." He set forth in search of the precious bag. All night he wandered through the forest, but could not find it. When the morning came, he went back to his wigwam and sat down to think what he was to do. "If I had my pipe," he said to himself, "I would not feel so sad."

As he sat there, he thought he heard a noise like the wolverine behind his lodge. Going out quickly, he saw the scamp among the trees. Wesakchak followed, but could see nothing more of the animal. He tramped on until he was tired, then turned homewards again.

As he was passing near a tall tree, he looked up, and there was his Fire Bag hanging from one of the highest branches. The tree was smooth and tall, and as Wesakchak began to climb he found himself slipping down very often. Then he would catch hold quickly with his feet and hands. After very hard work he succeeded at last in reaching the bag. Then he slid quickly down the tree. But when he looked up at it, he saw that its bark was hanging in torn pieces where he had caught it with his feet and hands. So, to this day, the tamarac bark hangs in tattered shreds to show that Wesakchak once climbed it.

On the way home he heard the wolverine, who was just trying to sneak away among the bushes.

"Come forth here, brother wolverine," called Wesakchak. "I want to talk to you."

The wolverine came out and stood in front of him. He did not look a bit sorry for what he had done.

"You are always getting into mischief," said Wesakchak. "Now, I am going to punish you for playing so many mean tricks. After this your legs will be very short and crooked, and you will not be able to run as fast as you did before."

As he said this, the wolverine's legs grew short and bent, and with an angry growl the animal disappeared among the trees.

A Wonderful Journey

One day Wesakchak decided to go on a long journey. He knew that somewhere, many miles away, there was a village where people lived, and he made up his mind to go and see them.

The birds all loved Wesakchak, so a great many of them had given him their feathers to make into a suit. When it was finished, it was very beautiful. The vest was of snow-white feathers from the pigeons' breasts, the coat, of shining blue ones, given by the bluebirds. The leggings were made of black and brown feathers, which the blackbirds and thrushes had gladly sent to him. Around his neck and wrists he put bright yellow feathers, the gift of the canaries. In his hair he wore the eagle's feathers, for he was a great chief.

He set off early one morning, and as he travelled on, the birds and animals whom he passed all spoke to him. By and by he met a prairie-chicken. In those days the prairie-chicken was a pale grey color.

"Good-morning, brother prairie-chicken," said Wesakchak. "I have been hearing strange tales about you. The animals tell me that you are very proud of the way that you can startle them."

"But I only remain still in the grass until they come close to me and then fly up suddenly," replied the prairie-chicken. "I do not mean to frighten them, but it is great fun to see them jump."

"That may be so," said Wesakchak. "But it is not kind of you to fly up in their faces. Then I hear that you are so proud of this, that you call yourself 'Kee-koo,' or the Startsome Bird."

The prairie-chicken did not reply to this, but remained still in the grass.

"Why do you not fly up in front of me?" asked Wesakchak. Still the prairie-chicken did not move or speak. Suddenly Wesakchak leaned down and gathered a handful of little stones.

"Start now," he said, as he threw them at the chicken. The small pebbles lit on its back and it flew up suddenly. The stones rolled off, but their marks remained, and so after that the prairie-chicken was always speckled.

Wesakchak continued his journey, and late in the afternoon he came to a creek. The water of the little stream was not clean enough to wade through, for green slime floated on the top and reeds grew in its boggy mud. It was rather too wide to jump, but Wesakchak decided to make a running jump and see if he could get across. He ran back a pace on the prairie, then forward to the bank, but the prairie-grass was so long that his feet became entangled, so he went back to start again. He did this two or three times, and at last had the grass packed down enough so that he could make a good run. Then he came forward at a great speed and made a leap. But just as he did so, the prairie-chicken flew up at his feet, and he fell face downwards in the swampy water.

Wesakchak was very vexed, and he called out to the prairie-chicken, "This is a mean trick you have played on me, and in punishment you shall not be able to fly very well after this." The prairie-chicken heard him and began to fly towards the forest, but its wings seemed shorter than they used to be and it fluttered away amid the tall grass.

As Wesakchak waded out through the reeds, each bent before him, making a path that has remained there ever since. When he reached the shore, it took him a long time to clean his beautiful suit, and by the time he was ready to go on, it was nearly evening. He was anxious to reach the village before nightfall, so he hurried on, wishing he could find some one to take him the rest of the way, for he was feeling tired.

After a time he came in sight of a little lake, and there saw two swans floating on the water. He called to them, but they did not seem to hear, so he jumped into the water and dove down to the bottom. Then he came up under the swans and caught each one by the legs. They flew up with him hanging to their feet.

"Take me to the village that is built on the river bank," Wesakchak said to them. They did not answer, but flew rapidly through the air.

After they had gone some miles, he noticed they were not taking the right direction. He called to them and told them to turn to the east, but they did not reply. When he saw they were not going to obey he hung on tightly by one hand, and reaching up, he caught one swan by the neck. He tried to pull its head down so that he could talk to it, but the harder he pulled, the firmer it held its head up, until at last its neck was turned into a curve. He then tried the other swan, but with no more success, so now both birds had their beautiful, white necks curved like the letter S. When Wesakchak saw they would not listen to him, and that they were taking him in the wrong direction, he let go his hold of their feet and dropped like a stone through the air. He landed on a hollow stump, and with such force that he sank deep into the soft wood. Not a sign of him could be seen; he had disappeared entirely. After some time two squaws came to get the soft, yellow wood from the stump. They use this wood to smoke their buckskins, because it gives the skin a nice color. They had brought axes with them to chop down the stump. As they began chopping, they heard a noise like groans coming from within the stump. They were very frightened and thought it was a bear. Just as they were turning to run away Wesakchak called to them.

"It is no bear," said the first woman. "It is the wise man, Wesakchak, who is coming to visit us."

"It is, indeed, he," said the second woman. "We must chop him out."

So they set to work with their axes, and in a little while had chopped open the stump and set him free. They were overjoyed when they saw it was really Wesakchak whom they had freed, and they took him with them to the village, where all came forth to welcome him.

The Further Adventures of Wesakchak

The Grey Goose

Many years ago, when Wesakchak was the only man upon the earth, there was a being, the Evil Spirit, who did not love him. This spirit was very wicked, and when he saw how much the animals loved Wesakchak, he made up his mind to carry out a cunning scheme, for he wanted to become the master of the animals himself, and it made him very jealous to see how they obeyed Wesakchak.

But the North Wind, when it was passing by his wigwam, heard the Evil Spirit say what he was going to do. The wind passed on, and when it came to the birch-tree, it told her. She told it to her leaves, and they rustled in the wind, as they listened to the terrible plan. "Oh, North Wind," said the birch-tree, "will you carry my leaves to the wigwam of Wesakchak, and they will tell him of his danger?" So the North Wind took the dried leaves of the birch-tree and carried them many miles, until they reached the wigwam of Wesakchak. There it dropped them at his door.

Wesakchak was sitting by the fire, and he heard the rustling leaves. "Listen!" they said to him. "We have a message for you." Then they told him of the terrible plan the North Wind had overheard. It was in the spring the Evil Spirit was going to carry out his purpose.

Wesakchak hunted all winter in the forest. When spring came, he was near the edge of the woods one day, and as he stepped out into the prairie, he heard a little rustle at his feet. He looked down and saw some leaves of the birch-tree. "Remember the message we carried to you, O Master," they said. Wesakchak answered, "Yes, I remember. It is now spring, and I shall go back to my wigwam for my bow and arrows. Then I shall go in search of the Evil Spirit, my enemy."

The next day Wesakchak left his lodge and travelled over the prairie. Towards nightfall he reached a low valley. He saw that the snow was melting and that some feet of water lay in the valley. But he did not stop for this. He walked on through the water, never resting even when the darkness descended. But when the sun rose next morning, he saw that the plan of the Evil Spirit was being carried out, for all around him lay water. The Evil Spirit had melted the snow during the night, and now every little stream was swollen as big as a river, and the valley was full of water to the brim.

Wesakchak had to swim, and after he had gone some miles, he began to feel very tired. Then the jackfish swam up to him and said, "My Master, get on my back and I shall take you safely to the land." Wesakchak at once did as he was told, and the jackfish, who was strong and a swift swimmer, soon brought him safely to the dry land.

Then Wesakchak went home to his lodge. It was not far away, and he could see it rising out of the water like an island, for the land on which it was built was a tiny hill. He was very glad to be inside his wigwam and to sit down beside the fire; but as he looked out through the open door, he saw the water rising steadily, and knew that by morning it would be in his lodge, and that he, if no help came, would be drowned.

Wesakchak was very tired, and as he sat there thinking, he fell asleep, and he had a strange dream. He thought Nihka, the wild goose, flew into the wigwam and around and around near the top, flapping her wings and crying. She seemed to say, "Give me a message! Give me a message! And I shall save you." Around and around she flew, and at last lighted in the ashes of the smouldering fire and disappeared.

Then Wesakchak wakened, and as he looked around the wigwam, he knew that Nihka must have been there, for everything had fallen on the floor as if struck by her wings, and the floor of the lodge was covered with ashes. The fire was out, and in the centre of it lay the quill of a goose. Wesakchak picked it up, and saw that a little piece of birch bark was rolled inside. He pulled it out, and as he did so, he heard the honk-honk of a wild goose, and Nihka flew in at the door.

"Write on the birch bark," she said, "and I shall take it to your friend the beaver."

Wesakchak did as she told him. He wrote a message on the birch bark and slipped it in the hollow end of the quill. As he gave it to Nihka, he saw that she was no longer white as she had been, but was grey with the ashes of the fire, and marked with black specks where the cinders had touched her. Her breast was still white, and a small patch under her wings.

Nihka took the quill and flew off at once. It was not long before Wesakchak saw the beaver coming to him through the water. When he came close, Wesakchak saw that he carried mud in his paws and on his broad, flat tail. When he reached the door of the lodge, he put the mud down and patted it smooth and hard with his tail. Then he swam away and brought back more, and this he did until he had made a path across the water. Wesakchak had stood watching the beaver as he worked, and now as it was finished, he said:

"Brother Beaver, this is a wonderful bridge you have made for me. How did you learn to do it? Surely the Great Spirit has taught you this, to make a path of land in the midst of the water."

"Yes, Master," answered the beaver, "the Great Spirit has taught me how to do this, that you might escape the wicked snares of your enemy. If you cross to the other side, you will be safe."

"Thank you, Brother Beaver," said Wesakchak, "I shall do as you say," and stepping out on the mud bridge, he walked safely to dry land.

Then, in memory of this kindness, Wesakchak told the beaver that from that time he might always build a path across the water to remind his children of what he had done. Then, turning to the goose, he told her that he wished her to wear always her dress of grey and black, so that the world might not forget her loving service.

Each spring, the Evil Spirit, who is the spring flood, grows wild with rage, as he remembers how his plan was spoiled, and he tries to waste the lands of Wesakchak and his children. But this is always in vain, for the Evil One can never win.

Little Brother Rabbit

One autumn Wesakchak felt very sad. All through the summer there had been no rain. The prairie grass was burnt brown and dry. The little streams had grown smaller and narrower, until at last not a drop of water was left. The animals, finding no grass to eat and no water to drink, had all gone to the far north-west, where the Great River came down from the mountains. For they knew that along its banks they would find grass to eat. Wesakchak wondered if the Great Spirit were angry with the people of the plains when He sent them these long, hot days and nights. Why did He let the animals go away from them, leaving the hunters no game to kill? The little children were crying for food, and the warriors had grown thin and sad during this summer. And now the fever had come, and in the lodges many sick were lying.

Wesakchak felt that he must do something for his people, so he asked the Great Spirit to show him where the animals lived, so that he might tell his hunters and save the lives of all in the tribe. Then Wesakchak took his canoe and carried it until he came to the Great River. Getting in, he paddled for many days and many nights. He watched all the time, to see if any game came near the banks, but he saw no sign of any.

At last, after he had gone many hundreds of miles, he felt so tired that he knew he must rest. He drew his canoe up to the side of the river and made a lodge from the branches of trees. Here he slept during the night, and when morning came, he arose quite rested. Before he had gone to sleep that night he had noticed that the clouds hung low, and he had wondered if there would be snow in the morning. Now, when he came forth from his lodge, he saw that all the land was white. During the night a heavy fall of soft snow had come, and all the trees and the prairie were covered with it.

Wesakchak was greatly pleased, for this was just what he had hoped for. Now he would be able to see the marks of the animals and trace them to their homes. Going down to the river, he was delighted to find the trail of deer, who had been down for a drink. There were also the marks of the other animals, and now Wesakchak made up his mind to follow these trails and find where the animals were living. He set out, and tramped for many miles. The sun arose and shone on the snow, making everything a dazzling white. But Wesakchak did not mind, and tramped on. At length he knew he was near the place where the animals were living. He took a good look at the trees, so that he could tell the hunters where to find them. Then he turned to hurry back, for he wished to let them know as soon as possible. He tramped on again for a long time, but he did not seem to be getting any nearer to the river. He stopped and looked around. Everything was glistening white, and nowhere could he see a river or a tree. He wondered if he were lost and what he would do, for he knew that if the sick people did not get food soon, they would die. He turned in another direction and travelled for some time. Then stopping, he looked around once more. Again all was glistening white, dazzling his eyes so much that he could see nothing. He knew now that he was snowblind, and felt very sad indeed, for how could he get the news to the hunters in time to save the sick ones, when he could not find the river and his canoe? If only there was something to guide him, — some dark object that he could see; but everything was a dazzling whiteness.

Just then he noticed a little, brown object in front of him. As he looked at it, it hopped a few steps ahead and then stopped.

"Oh, Brother Rabbit," called Wesakchak, "I am so glad to see you. I cannot find the river and I want to get back and tell the hunters where the game is living."

"Let me guide you," said the rabbit. "Keep watching me, and you can see my dark fur against the white snow."

As he said this he hopped away, and Wesakchak, looking only at the little, dark body, was able to follow, till at last they reached the bank of the river. The canoe was there, and Wesakchak stepped in at once, glad that he would now be able to carry the good news to the warriors and hunters. Before he paddled away he turned to the rabbit and said:

"My little Brother Rabbit, you have been very kind to me, indeed, and through your kindness the lives of our tribe will be saved. In return for this your brown fur shall become white as the first snowfall, so that no one will be able to see your body against the snow. In this way you may protect yourself, and people will know how kind the rabbit was to Wesakchak."

As he spoke, the rabbit's fur suddenly became pure white, and it looked like a little ball of snow near the bushes. Wesakchak smiled when he saw this and said:

"Your enemies will need to have sharp eyes now, little Brother Rabbit, for you will give them many a long chase over the winter prairies."

The Bald-headed Eagles

One day Wesakchak was seated at the door of his lodge, when he noticed two eagles circling high in the air above him.

"Come down, my brothers," he called. "I wish to speak to you."

The eagles slowly descended, and Wesakchak said, "I wish you to take me on your backs for a ride. This is a very warm day and I know it must be cool high up in the air where you fly."

"But we are going home to our nest," replied the eagles. "It is on a very high cliff many miles from here, and you will not care to go there."

'Yes, I shall," replied Wesakchak. 'I should like to see your nest and your young eagles. Take me on your backs with you."

The eagles did not seem very eager to take him, but Wesakchak, without waiting for any more words, jumped on their backs, and they began to mount in the air. Up and up they went, until at last they were as high as the clouds. Wesakchak now began to feel rather cold and asked them to fly lower, but they gave him no answer. On and on they went, and Wesakchak clung tightly to their backs, for he felt very dizzy, being up so high in the air. At last he began to wonder where their nest could be, for he could see no sign of rocks or cliffs of any kind. After what seemed to be hours to him, the eagles began to descend, and in a few minutes they alighted on the top of a very high crag. Wesakchak slipped from their backs and looked around him. Near him was the nest of the eagles, and in it were the young, crying loudly for food.

Below, Wesakchak could see the ground, which seemed miles away; above him the clouds, which looked low and stormy. The eagles fed their young, and after Wesakchak had waited awhile he said, "Now, my brothers, please take me to my home."

"You are tired of our cliff?" asked the eagles: "Well, you must go home yourself, for we are not going away for some hours."

"Oh, I cannot stay here that long," said Wesakchak. "Besides, I am tired and very hungry, and there is nothing here but bare rock. You must take me home."

The eagles did not dare to disobey Wesakchak, so they let him mount on their backs. Then they began to fly slowly away. After a while it seemed to him that they were going in the wrong direction. He could see snow-capped mountains, and, as his lodge was built on the prairies, he said:

"My brothers, you are not taking me to my lodge. You are going in the wrong direction. Turn and fly the other way." But the eagles, instead of answering, only flew more rapidly towards the mountains. Again Wesakchak called to them and again they did not reply. He now saw that they did not intend to take him home, and he began to wonder what he could do.

In a few moments the eagles slowly circled around the top of a mountain from whose summit a large piece of ice was just ready to slip. When the eagles were directly above the ice, they suddenly turned with a jerk and hurled Wesakchak from their backs. Down, down he fell, alighting on the ice, which at once slipped from its place and began to descend the mountain side with terrible rapidity. Wesakchak clung desperately to the icy block, and felt himself going with it and the loose pieces of rock and the small trees which it uprooted on its way. As they came down, the speed became greater, until at last they were bounding over huge stones and across chasms, and with one terrible leap Wesakchak flew through the air and alighted on the ground at the foot of the mountain. Behind them their pathway down the mountain side was marked by a deep ravine cut in the rocky sides of the hill. And around Wesakchak lay ice and stones and uprooted trees.

He lay perfectly still, for he was rendered insensible with the terrible force with which he had fallen. After several hours he opened his eyes, but was too weak to move. He could hear the voices of two wolves near him. One was saying, "He is dead. Let us go and eat him, for I am very hungry." Then the other wolf answered, "No, he is not dead, and I think he is Wesakchak, for look, see his suit made of the feathers of birds. It is only Wesakchak who has a suit like that."

Wesakchak heard all this, but he could not move or speak.

As he lay there with his eyes open, he noticed two eagles circling high in the air above him. This aroused him, and he called to the wolves in a faint voice, "My brothers, come near to me." The wolves seemed surprised, but they came slowly to his side.

"You were arguing a moment ago as to whether I was dead," said Wesakchak to them. "Now you can see I am not dead, but I wish you to pretend to be eating me, for I want those eagles to come down, and if they think I am dead, they will come so that they can make a meal off me, too."

The wolves did as he asked them and pretended to be eating him. When the eagles saw this, they hovered lower for a moment or two, then darted down. Wesakchak was lying with his two arms stretched out at full length, and now the eagles began to peck at the palms of his hands. At once he grabbed them by the feathers on their heads.

"Now I have you," he said. "You shall be punished for playing such a trick as this on me."

The eagles pulled desperately to try and get away, and Wesakchak clung just as desperately to their heads. At last, with one mighty jerk, they pulled their heads free, but Wesakchak still held the feathers in his hands and their heads were bald.

"This shall be your punishment, then," said Wesakchak, very sternly. "From this day you and all your race shall have no feathers on your heads, so that every one may know how unkind you have been to Wesakchak."

And so it has been. From that day the two eagles and all their children have been bald-headed.

Pronouncing Vocabulary

The following signs for the variation of the sound of "a" are used in the vocabulary:

ā to denote the long sound.
ă to denote the short sound.
ȧ to denote the sound as in pȧst.
ä to denote the sound as in stär.
ạ to denote the sound as in bạll.

For e:
ē to denote the long sound.
ĕ to denote the short sound.
ẽ to denote the sound as in hẽr.

For i:
ī to denote the long sound.
ĭ to denote the short sound.

For o:
ō to denote the long sound.
ŏ to denote the short sound.

For u:
ū to denote the long sound.
ŭ to denote the short sound.

ȧ ė ȯ are similar in sound to ā ē ō, but are not so long.

Anishinaba (ă-nĭsh′-ĭn-ă-bȧ).
Aseelkwa (ȧ-sēēl′-kwa).
Assiniboine (ȧ-sĭn-ĭ-bo̱in).
Azhabee (ăz′-hă-bēē).
Beauman (bō′-man).
Bokwewa (bŏk′-wē-wạ).
Chippewa (chĭp′-ĕ-wạ).
Gitche Manitou (git′chē man′-ĭ-to͞o).
Hahola (hă′-hō-la).
Iroquois (ĭr-ō-kwa).
Kabibonokka (kȧ-bĭb′-ō-nōk-kă).
Kasamoldin (kăs′-ă-mōld-ĭn).
Kee-Koo (kēē′-koo).

Koto (kō'-tō).
Lalita (lă-lēēt'-ă).
Lemichin (lĕ-mĭch'-ĭn).
Mackinac (măk-ĭn-ăc).
Manitoline (man'-ĭ-tōōl-in).
Manitou (man'-ĭ-tōō).
Masswaweinini
(măss-wą-wē-nĭnnē').
Milkanops (mĭlk'-ă-nŏps).
Mishini-Makinak
(măsh-ĭn-ī-mak-in-ak).
Moowis (moo'-wĭs).
Mudjekeewis (mŭd-jĕ-kē'-wĭs).
Negahnahbee (nĕg-ă-nȧ'-bē).
Nicolas (nĭk'-ō-lȧs).
Nihka (nē'-kȧ).
Odjibaa (ō'-jĭ-bą).
Ojeeg (ō'-jēēg).
Okanagan (ō'-kȧn-ą-gȧn).
Onawataquto (ŏn-a-wą-tă-qu'-tō).
Onwe Bahmondoong
(ŏn'-wē bă'-mŏn-doong).
Osages (ŏ'-sāges).
Saultaux (sal-tō).
Shingebiss (shĭng'-ĕ-bĭs).
Shuswaps (shū-swăp).
Sinikielt (sin'-ĭ-kēēlt).
Sioux (sū).
Tserman (tĕrs-man).
Wagemena (wag'-a-mēnă).
Wampum (wȧm-pŭm).
Wasbashas (wăs-băs'-hăs).
Waupee (wą'-pēē).
Weeng (wēēng).
Wesakchak (wē'-să-k-chak).